I0453095

Tuesdays with Molakesh the Destroyer

and Other Tales

Tuesdays with Molakesh the Destroyer

and Other Tales

MEGAN GREY

GARDEN NINJ BOOKS

TUESDAYS WITH MOLAKESH THE DESTROYER
AND OTHER TALES
Copyright © 2016 by Megan Grey

Cover Design by Holly Heisey
Cover image by Galen Dara
Author photo by Heather Palmer Cavill

Published by Garden Ninja Books

MeganGrey.com

First Edition: March 2016

0 9 8 7 6 5 4 3 2 1

For Glen,
who knew I was a writer
and married me anyway

Table of Contents

Tuesdays With Molakesh the Destroyer

Molakesh the Destroyer moved into the house next door the summer I turned fifteen. There was the expected neighborhood gossip at first, with Mom and her friends worrying about what having a demon on our street might do for property values and with one particularly zealous neighbor lining her property with crosses, but it died down after a few months. Destroyer he may be called, but he kept his yard tidy and pulled in his trash cans at night, so the Homeowners Association turned their scowls on other targets.

For my part, I didn't care who we shared a fence line with and pretty much forgot he existed. Until two days after the first winter snowstorm.

"You should shovel Molakesh's driveway," Mom said, peering out through the blinds of the kitchen window.

I looked up from my phone. "What?"

"There's at least two feet of snow out there."

"He's a demon, Mom."

Mom turned away from the window and opened the fridge. She rustled through produce bags and pulled out two large bell peppers. "Yes, but he's old and there's no way he'll be able to get out of his driveway. I'm sure he doesn't have snow tires."

"Seriously? I just got home from school and now you want me to go to the demon's house and—"

"It's called service, Sarah Jean." She set the peppers down on a wooden cutting board. She'd sauté them with onions, the only way she ever cooked bell peppers. I hated them, but my opinion was never taken into account in meal planning.

"It's called insanity."

Mom raised an eyebrow, the knife hovering above the pepper, and I knew what was coming next. "You can either practice service by shoveling our neighbor's driveway, or you can spend tonight writing an essay on ten reasons why service is important."

I groaned. "Fine. I'll shovel his stupid driveway."

Mom smiled and began chopping. "I knew you'd come around."

I bundled up in my thick coat and gloves, then pulled on snowboots still coated in slush from my walk home from school. She didn't even notice my parting glare as I stomped out of the house.

I grabbed our snow shovel and crunched through the yard toward Molakesh's driveway, all the while composing an essay in my head titled "Ten Reasons Why Parents Suck."

I paused just past his front window. The ever-present dark green curtains hung perfectly still, but I could have sworn I saw them shift out of the corner of my eye.

The snow on the driveway was pristine white and powdery, without a single set of tire-tracks marring the surface. I didn't know if Mom was right about him not having snow tires — if a demon could buy groceries at Hal's like the rest of us, I didn't see why he couldn't hit up an auto shop — but it was obvious he hadn't left his house since the storm.

My shovel scraped along the concrete as I worked, pushing the snow into huge piles framing the driveway. I had done about a quarter of it when the front door opened and Molakesh poked his horned head out.

"What do you think you're doing out there?" he demanded.

I only barely managed to keep from gaping. I'd seen Molakesh a couple times before around town, but the sight wasn't exactly one you get used to. His face was every bit as wrinkled and patchy as my eighty-seven-year-old grandpa, and his steel-gray eyebrows almost as long, but the resemblance didn't go much further. Curved horns about six inches long sprouted from a pockmarked head lined with wispy white hairs. Large red eyes blazed contempt from deep sockets, and his mouth hung far lower on his face than any human's did, making it look like his jaw might snap off in a stiff breeze.

"Well? Answer me!" he said.

"I'm, uh . . . I'm shoveling."

Those red eyes didn't so much as blink.

"Your driveway. For you," I continued, speaking slower. I hadn't heard he was an idiot as well as a fiend of hell.

He stepped out from behind the doorway. He wore brown old man pants — "slacks," my grandpa called them — and a threadbare navy-blue cardigan with sleeves ending far short of his claws. Those claws wrapped around themselves in what appeared to be the demon approximation of clenched fists.

"Do you think I have no powers left? Do you think Molakesh the Destroyer cannot burn the snow from his own driveway? Do you think I cannot rain fire upon this entire worthless town?"

I looked around at the snow-covered houses, at the thick icicles hanging from every eave and the piles of slush that sprayed from the wheels of a passing car. I doubted Satan himself could burn Winslow, Minnesota, down.

"Whatever," I said, and started back to my house. The essay was sounding better and better.

Those red eyes followed me in silence as I made my way around the piles I'd created and back the way I'd come. I was just about to cross onto our property when Molakesh spoke again.

"Wait! Stop!"

I sighed. It misted out in front of me. "What? I was just trying to help, you know. Service."

Molakesh continued to stare. Then: "I believe you humans offer your servants hot chocolate on cold days."

"I said 'service'. That doesn't make me your servant."

Molakesh made a growling noise in his throat like the rumble of the morning school bus. "You served me, so I'm going to make you hot chocolate. Come here."

I looked back to my house. I couldn't see my mom through the blinds. Would she be more upset if I went in the demon's house or if I refused his offer of hot chocolate? Either way, it could mean incurring her wrath, and now that I was only months away from getting my drivers' license, she had a more potent threat than essays to lord over me.

"Fine," I said after a minute. "But on your porch, not in your house. I don't know what you do in there, but I'm not going to be your child bride or virgin sacrifice or anything. I'm not even a virgin." That was a lie, but I figured it couldn't hurt.

He blinked and went back into his house, slamming the door behind him. I crunched back through the snow yet again to his porch. I waited for several minutes, stamping snow from my boots and debating whether a particularly wicked-looking icicle could be used as a demon-slaying weapon if necessary.

The door swung open and Molakesh emerged with two steaming mismatched mugs in his claws. One had the University of Minnesota logo on it and the other a picture of Tweety Bird. He handed me the Tweety Bird one.

I sniffed it, eyeing him warily over the rim of the cup for sudden movements. The drink looked and smelled like hot chocolate. One lone marshmallow floated on top.

"Hal's store brand," Molakesh said.

I took a sip. So it was.

"Uh, thanks."

Molakesh did not drink his. "You would never do as a sacrifice anyway."

I frowned. "Why not?"

He pointed at my face with one of his claws. "Your blemish. I like my sacrifices unstained."

"It's a birthmark," I snapped. I got enough crap from kids at school about the dark patch extending from my left cheekbone to the corner of my mouth. I sure as hell didn't need to take any from some ancient demon.

"I was referring to your acne."

"Oh." This probably shouldn't have made me feel better, but it did.

"You don't like your birthmark?"

"I don't have a problem with it. But some of the kids at school do."

"What do they say about it?"

I scowled down at the hot chocolate. The marshmallow bobbed forlornly on top. "They call me Shit-face."

Molakesh made an odd noise, which I realized was a chuckle. It turned into a cough, though, and he doubled over against the wooden porch railing, hacking his lungs out. Possibly literally. Something pink and gross flew from his mouth and landed in the snow.

"Are you . . . are you all right?" My thoughts on icicles as weapons aside, Mom definitely wouldn't let me get my drivers' license if Molakesh died as a result of my shoddy conversational skills.

"Yes, yes," he wheezed. He set his half-spilled mug of hot chocolate on the railing. "I may not have the vigor I once had, but a single laugh at another's misfortune won't be the end of me."

I kind of doubted it. For all his previous ranting on how he would burn down the whole town, just then he looked about as fragile as my grandpa, who Mom kept saying wouldn't last until the next holiday.

And yet somehow, he always did.

"So you think that's funny?" I asked.

"What I find amusing is the sheer lack of creativity in children today. I would have taunted you with something so vile, so inescapable, you would have ripped that birthmark from your face with your own hands." He looked wistful. "But that was in another time."

I tried to imagine what would possibly inspire that kind of reaction in a person. I supposed Shit-face was rather pedestrian compared to what an actual demon could come up with.

"Maybe you can use that creativity of yours on Katelyn Sams." She was the worst of them. I wouldn't mind seeing her rip some of that pretty blonde hair out of her head.

Those too-low lips twisted into a sneer. "I don't take requests. Especially not from *teenagers.*" He made the last word sound like a worse epithet than Shit-face.

"It's not like I was serious," I muttered. "So do you want me to finish the driveway or not?"

Molakesh regarded me for a moment, then waved a claw dismissively. "If you must." He picked up the barely-touched mugs of hot chocolate and went back inside, slamming the door behind him.

I hefted my shovel and returned to the driveway, doing the bare minimum needed for that rusty old Cadillac of his to be able to make it to the street. The curtains stirred again as I worked, and I flipped him off before returning home.

Another snowstorm blew in that weekend, and the next Tuesday I was over at Molakesh's house again with a snow shovel, cursing the icy wind and my mom's service kick and Katelyn Sams for good measure.

This time Molakesh stood on the porch and glared at me while I worked. He held the University of Minnesota mug. The Tweety Bird mug sat on the railing, the steam tugged away from it by the wind.

I finished and set the shovel against the ice-slick porch steps. "I thought you said you had powers. Rain of fire and all that. So why don't you ever take care of your own damn driveway?" Mom would kill me if she heard me talk this way to any adult, even a demonic one, but the guy wasn't exactly bursting with politeness himself.

"You doubt my powers?"

I drank the hot chocolate too fast; it burned my tongue, but warmed my throat nicely. "I guess."

He stared out over the white landscape. The wind gusted more snow back to where I had just shoveled, but I would write ten essays on service before I was going to shovel his driveway twice in the same day.

Then he held out his right claw, with the sharp points I couldn't help but think of as fingers curved upwards. A ball of fire appeared, floating inches above in the air. His eyes glowed as bright orange as the fire, though of their own accord or due to the reflected light, I couldn't say. Even his horns seemed sharper, deadlier.

I took a step back, my eyes wide, as he tossed the fire at the yard with the smooth, practiced motion of a major league pitcher. A trail of flames streaked across the yard as the ball hit, leaving behind a long, deep rut of exposed dirt and blackened grass as the fire died down.

"Whoa," I said. "That was—"

Molakesh began coughing again like before, only worse. His long-limbed body, which had appeared unnaturally tall and strong only thirty seconds before, sagged in on itself. He collapsed to his knees.

I reached for his arm instinctively, trying to hold him up, but he shoved me back. Hot chocolate splashed out of my mug and melted through the snow on the porch.

"Get away from me," he growled. Another piece of that disgusting fleshy pink hung from his lips.

"Fine." I set the mug on the porch next to him and grabbed my shovel.

He pulled himself up to the railing, leaning against it as if that was the only thing holding him up. He stared out at the trail of burned snow. I wasn't particularly good at reading normal people's expressions, let alone demons', but he looked weary. And not just physically.

"That was cool, though," I called when I reached my own front porch, my gloved hand on the doorknob.

He didn't make any indication he'd heard me. He just kept staring.

Three gray weeks passed, the snow on the sidewalks and streets packing harder and harder until sheets of treacherous ice slicked over everything. When snow fell once more, bringing a welcome traction on my walk back from school, I passed Molakesh's house with only a single glance. The snow had filled that burned-out rut in the front yard.

Mom told me to go shovel his driveway again, but I wrote the stupid essay instead. Then I made the mistake of going online. Katelyn and her cronies had created a fake profile for me, where they posted badly spelled rants about how ugly I was, along with photoshopped pictures of me with a steaming turd on my cheek. Half the school had joined in, it seemed, leaving post after vicious post. I wanted to rip up my useless essay on service. Instead, I made myself a cup of hot chocolate and imagined the heat in my hand was an orb of fire.

I imagined the faces of the kids at school who called me Shit-face and left bags of dog poop in my locker. I imagined their terror as the school burned down around them.

So you're, like, retired, right? Why did you pick here?" I folded my legs up under me, sitting cross-legged as best as possible in the wicker chair Molakesh had dragged out onto the porch when he saw me walking to school. I would be late, but even hanging out with a creepy old demon was better than first period German. And Frau Witner was so blind, she wouldn't even notice I wasn't there. The chair creaked under me as I shifted.

Molakesh glowered at me. "Why can't you sit like a normal person?"

"What? This is normal. And why can't you answer a simple question?"

He leaned back in his own wicker chair, his legs crossed almost daintily at the ankles. His cloven goat hooves no longer looked so odd to me, but old man or not, he really needed to do something about those lame brown pants.

"I didn't pick here. I was sent here. A joke, I suppose. He always had a particularly vile sense of humor." Molakesh's claws clinked against the ceramic mug.

I didn't bother asking who "he" was. Some higher-level demon or Satan himself, it didn't really matter.

"A joke?"

"I am — was — a fire demon, formed from the fiery pits of hell. Born in flame, to die in… this." He gestured to the bleak snowy landscape. His red eyes glowed dimly, like the last embers twitching under banked coal.

"Winslow's not so bad."

"Says Shit-face herself."

He was right. I hated it here. I shrugged. "I only have a few more years left and then I can leave for college. Maybe go to Arizona. Or Florida, where my dad lives."

"Your dad who sends you a card for your birthday and Christmas, but otherwise pretends you don't exist?"

"What, are you going through our mail now?"

His long saggy lips twitched up into a smile. "I don't need to. I've been a demon for hundreds of years. Teenage angst is, as you humans say, our 'bread and butter.'"

I sipped more hot chocolate. He'd added some cinnamon this time, which tasted weird. But I didn't want to go to school yet, so I sat and drank.

"So what do retired demons do anyway? There has to be more to your life than making hot chocolate and annoying me."

"Sadly, not much."

"Really? Don't you occasionally, you know, cause strife in the hearts of man? Maybe a curse or two every once in awhile?" I pictured Katelyn Sams again, her perfectly arched eyebrows falling off in the middle of cheer practice. Or maybe growing thick and bushy, turning into two fat, squirming caterpillars above her blue eyes. I smiled into my hot chocolate.

"Let me guess. You have a few names in mind?"

"Maybe," I said, trying to sound casual.

"Too bad. You'll have to take your own revenge, as pathetic as that will likely be. I am no longer in possession of my former powers. All I have left is what I showed you, a mere hint of my previous glory. I am a useless shell, left out here to perish. In *Minnesota*." He swirled the liquid around in his mug. He wasn't drinking much today. He could probably use something a whole lot stronger than Hal's hot chocolate.

"I don't know. That fireball was pretty sweet." I didn't know why I wanted to comfort Molakesh. He was a demon, after all. The Destroyer. Who knew what kind of horrible crap he'd pulled in his undoubtedly long lifetime? But I kept thinking of my grandpa, a husk of a man being spoon-fed pudding by a nurse while blankly watching "The Price is Right" on a flickering old TV.

"Would you like it?" That horned head swiveled up from regarding the mug in his claws, his red eyes fixed intently on me.

"A fireball? What the hell would I do with a fireball?" I tried to push down the fiendish satisfaction I'd taken in imagining the school in flames, my poop-stinking locker reduced to ashes.

"Whatever you wish. The power of demon fire would be yours to control. You are young, fresh. It would be more powerful in you than even I could produce. Just a one-time use, mind you. You are human, after all. More than that would kill you."

I eyed the patch of yard where the deep rut in the ground was buried under snow. Then I stood up. The wicker chair creaked again, as if glad to be free of my weight. "I'm late for school."

"Enjoy your day, Shit-face."

My gloved hands clenched into fists. "Why would you give me something like that anyway?"

He stared at me, unblinking. "Because I have no one else to give anything to."

I sighed, watching the mist of my chocolate-scented breath puff out in the icy air. "So how will I know how to use it?"

"You'll know."

I could feel Molakesh's fireball burning somewhere deep within my chest, a warmth bordering on the uncomfortable, except when I was outside and it was better than the best goose-down coat. It burned in me as I passed Katelyn and her sheep climbing into their new cars to drive home. It burned in me as I discovered that she and her friends had cut the bottom out of my backpack, forcing me to awkwardly carry my books the whole walk home. It burned in me as I slipped and fell on the ice, scattering books and papers all around me into the snow.

I held the fire close to my heart, imagining.

As I turned the corner onto my block, I noticed Molakesh's front door was open. Wind gusted it back and forth, and had knocked over the wicker chairs left out front from our conversation two days before.

"Molakesh?" I called, climbing the steps to the porch. I pushed the door all the way open with my shoulder, my arms full of wet books. "You okay?"

No answer.

I walked in, trailing slush onto the ugly gray shag carpet. The air was as cold inside as out. I eyed a mirror hanging above a plain wooden entryway table. My birthmark looked redder than usual, angrier.

I set my books down on the table and walked into the living room. The only furniture sitting there was a threadbare, patched armchair in front of one of those ancient blocky TVs. Eerily similar to my grandpa's set-up in the nursing home, except for one thing.

Molakesh had candles of all sizes and colors, on every surface. None were lit, but the wicks were all blackened with use, and puddles of cold wax coated the carpet, the top of the TV, the kitchen table. He may have been a demon, but I knew instinctively the candles weren't for any satanic ritual. They were a reminder. A pitiful attempt of a used-up demon in a northern Minnesotan winter to surround himself with flame.

An empty pot sat on the stove. Two packets of Hal's hot chocolate lay on the counter next to it, along with our two mugs. Cleaned and waiting.

The only thing keeping my insides unfrozen was the ball of fire in my chest, flickering uncertainly.

"Molakesh?" I called again, though I knew there would be no answer, even before I found his body lying unmoving and cold in the twin-sized bed in the center of his otherwise empty bedroom. Empty except, of course, for dozens of unlit candles lining the walls. His eyes were open to the white ceiling, the red in them completely gone.

A one-time use, Molakesh had said of the gift he'd given me. I thought one last wistful time of Katelyn

Sams and her cronies coming out of the school, their mocking laughter turned to screams as flames erupted from my hands and torched her shiny new car right there in the parking lot. I thought of them sobbing and running and never daring to so much as look at me ever again.

Winslow sucked, but I would leave it all behind one day. I'd leave behind Shit-face, leave behind essay-writing punishments and bell peppers with dinner, leave behind winters that stretched on endlessly.

And now Molakesh could, too.

The fire came to me when I wished it, just as Molakesh had said it would. A ball of flame hovered above my hand. I wasn't practiced at throwing like he'd been, but it didn't seem to matter. When the fireball hit his body, the flames erupted upward, blackening the ceiling, spreading outward to catch the carpeting.

The heat seared my face and choked me, but I stayed just long enough to see his body totally consumed in flame. Before I left the house, I grabbed the two mugs and carried them home on top of my pile of books. I was halfway back to my house when I heard the massive crack of the bedroom collapsing in on itself.

I called 911 when I got home, then microwaved myself a cup of hot chocolate. Mom wouldn't be home from work for another hour or so yet, so she'd miss the show. The wail of approaching sirens sounded as I settled myself onto our porch with the Tweety Bird mug. I watched the flames shoot upwards from my demon neighbor's house, gorgeous threads of red and orange against a gray winter sky.

Molakesh would have liked it.

Missing

Imagine you're six and a half years old. The extra half makes a big difference, because it means you're that much closer to being one of the big kids. The ones who can stay up late and ride their bikes to school and who know all the jokes with words you don't understand and get in trouble for saying. Your world is all warm hugs and juice boxes and glittery gowns, movies where the princesses' dreams always come true and where no problem is too big to solve in ninety minutes, provided you've got a few talking animals to help.

Imagine you're at a street festival with your best friend and her family, eyes wide at all the colors and sounds, breathing in the scent of grilling meat mixed with the sugar-sweet aroma of funnel cakes and cotton candy. You hold hands with her, because that's what best friends do and because the crowd makes you nervous. But she's not afraid. She laughs at the performers and twirls in her pink tulle skirt she wears over purple leggings. You watch a man turn long balloons into animals with just a few twisty squeaks, and your friend's parents buy one for each of you. Yours is a yellow dog with big floppy ears. Your friend gets a pink unicorn, and now you wish you had a unicorn instead.

Imagine you see a carousel with all kinds of fantastical creatures bobbing up and down in a whirl of colors and tinkling music. You point it out to your friend, who squeals in joy. Her parents are busy buying food for her older brother, a boy who smells like dirt and corn chips, and don't see you and your friend run to get a closer view of the carousel. You think that maybe if you get there first, you'll get to ride the unicorn and this time she'll get stuck with the dog.

Imagine as you clutch the metal rails around the outside of the carousel, a man speaks from behind you.

"Excuse me, little girl. I think you dropped this." He holds out the yellow balloon dog you dropped during the run.

You and your friend both know that talking to strangers is wrong. But your friend has always been more daring than you, and when you take a step backwards, she takes one forward. "I have a unicorn," she says proudly, showing her pink balloon creation.

"Is that so?" the man asks. He has a pleasant smile.

"The dog is hers."

He holds it out. You only have to grab it, but you take another step back instead.

Your friend, who usually takes the lead in all social situations, reaches for it.

Imagine the last sight you have of your best friend is a flurry of pink skirt and purple leggings as she tries to kick free of the arms that grab her. The last sound you hear is one solitary shriek, drowned out in the screams from a nearby roller coaster. The man and your friend disappear, and all that is left is a pink balloon unicorn lying in the dirt. You don't want it anymore.

I don't have to imagine all of this, because I remember it. Every detail of that day, except for one thing. I can never picture the man's face. I couldn't then, couldn't tell the police any more than that he had a nice-man smile, and even now in my mind his face is a blank. Except for that smile. Pleasant. Normal. No sharp teeth or evil laugh that I'd expect from a monster.

My mom has spent hundreds of dollars—maybe thousands, I don't know—in therapy costs to convince me that Hayley's kidnapping wasn't my fault. But the truth of it is, I never thought it was.

It's just my fault she was never found.

Butterflies and Rotting Roses

From a shadowed corner in the back of the great hall, Enric could see that the Winter-height banquet had thus far failed to meet any of the guests' high expectations. The spread of food was modest, given the year's pittance of a harvest, and the musicians second-rate. Nobility gathered about in little clusters like birds, some occasionally flitting off to another flock to smile coolly and trade pleasant banter. Baron Veldenthane kept the red wine and spiced cider flowing, which no doubt helped, but Enric read the disappointment in their faces as the night wore on. Many of them had traveled for a week or more to arrive tonight, hoping to see the yearly display put on by the baron's skilled young illusive, and a few evergreen garlands and platters of roast duck alone were not worth their trouble.

None of this bothered Enric. His illusions could make the banquet appear as lush as the Queen's own, with silks and jewels and floating orbs of light, but he needed to conserve his energy. For this banquet, he had promised the baron something special.

He waited for the right moment, gauging the flow of the crowd and the hum of indistinct conversation. When a wide enough space toward the middle of the great hall cleared, Enric smiled. An enormous reptilian head burst through the stones of the floor, breathing a spurt of flames.

The guests screamed, terrified and thrilled all at once, as they jumped reflexively out of the way of the crackling fire and scattered chunks of granite, forgetting in the excitement that both would have passed through them like smoke. The dragon's claws scraped the stone with a shrill screech as it pulled the rest of its thick body from the ground, and the red scales covering it glistened like rubies in the light of the candles and its own flames.

The guests covered their ears, many flinching at the creature's echoing roar. One young woman reached out to touch the line of dragon's fire scorching across the table in front of her. She laughed delightedly, undoubtedly because of the actual warmth emanating from the illusion. Not many illusives could do sounds convincingly, and even fewer could have created a sense of real heat from the flames.

But he wasn't done yet.

Enric pulled the next image from his mind, a warrior clad in silver armor and a tunic bearing Veldenthane's colors of moss green and dark blue. The square-jawed hero stepped onto a bench, and a portly earl and his wife nearly fell to the ground in their scramble to get out of his way. The warrior vaulted over the table to cheers and gasps, swinging his sword at the great beast, who bathed the crowd once more in flames that would feel to them like a warm mist. The beast roared in defiance as the blade scored scaled flesh and sent droplets of black blood hissing onto the stone floor.

Enric clenched his jaw against the growing strain of the illusion. Sweat beaded on his forehead as the dragon lunged forward, and the warrior dodged just in time to avoid being split in two. Cries of surprise and encouragement filled the air. One noblewoman fainted into the arms of her companion.

The warrior wasted no opportunity. With a shout of righteous fury, he swung his sword once more, completely severing the beast's neck. The large head hit the floor, and the hall rang with the exultant cheers of banquet guests.

After saluting the crowd, the warrior bowed before Baron Veldenthane and his wife. He directed a deeper bow toward their niece, Azhlyn, who blushed a smear of pink, and smiled.

Enric released the image, breathing heavily. The warrior and decapitated dragon vanished, along with all traces of their existence.

"Let the dancing begin!" Baron Veldenthane shouted, prompting another round of cheers and applause from the now-eager guests. He clapped Enric on the back in passing, and led his wife out to the floor as lutes and drums sounded.

Enric was glad to have the gratitude of the baron, but it was Azhlyn whose reaction he truly cared about. Always Azhlyn, and no one else. She was the only reason an illusive of his abilities was still working for a backwater barony in the middle of Grimweth when he could be earning far more as a battle-illusive. Once word of the spectacular detail and size of this illusion got out, Enric wouldn't be surprised if the Queen herself sent an inquiry for his services.

But as his heart palpitated under Azhlyn's coy gaze, Enric knew he wouldn't even consider such an offer. Not yet. Not until his pledge was accepted by Veldenthane, who'd been her guardian since the death of her father three years prior.

"Quite extraordinary, young man," said Count Divstan, coming up from behind him. The count gripped Enric's hand and pumped it boisterously. Enric forced a smile. He wasn't a social man by nature, and the proximity of the count's drink-reddened face to his own made him uncomfortable. Besides, a headache was starting to bloom at the back of his skull from the exertion of the illusion, and Enric couldn't afford to lose focus.

Not tonight.

"Thank you," Enric murmured, carefully eyeing the swirl of colors as the rest of the attendees joined the dance. Azhlyn sat at the banquet table in the seat which once belonged to Baron Veldenthane's son, off serving as an officer in the queen's army. She sipped at her cider. Azhlyn would not be allowed to dance for another two months, when she was officially presented to the court and able to receive pledges.

At last.

He pulled back from the count, hoping to spare a moment to speak a bit with the girl he loved, perhaps manage more than his usual flustered greeting. Divstan, however, was not through.

"Every year, your display manages to top the year before! Who have you studied under? Bredgale? Norris, perhaps?" The count squinted, his lips pursed as he attempted to recall any other famous illusives from his sodden memory.

Enric barely refrained from rolling his eyes. *Norris? Ridiculous.* The man had been dead for twenty years. Enric had realized his gift early on, but that would be quite the stretch. "I worked for some time with the Guild," he said, "several years ba . . ."

His eye landed on something behind the count and his breath caught. A woman in blue silk stepped through the dance, her hand reaching for the baron's just as the partners were about to switch. It wasn't her beauty or grace that gave Enric a start, however. She rippled, as if he were seeing her underwater.

She was an illusion.

Count Divstan blanched, grabbed Enric's shoulder. "The Guild?" he squawked. A last attempt at distraction, perhaps, but too late.

"Baron! Get back!" yelled Enric, flinging his arm out toward the woman, who turned her face to him for a mere beat before lunging at Veldenthane. Enric focused, grabbed at the illusion, and clenched his fist—a useless crutch for an entirely mental motion, but that hardly mattered.

The façade of the woman crumpled away, blue silk becoming leather breeches and tunic, slender pale face shifting into a man's grizzled snarl. He held a blade in his hand and slashed at the baron, who had stumbled back at Enric's warning. Shrieks sounded in the hall again, this time filled with real fear. A woman near the doorway—an illusive Enric didn't recognize—fell to her knees, her hands cradling her head against the searing pain from an illusion ripped out of her control.

Guards rushed toward Veldenthane and tackled the assassin. The illusive, too, was easily apprehended by another set of guards before she could return to her feet. Enric looked back to where Count Divstan stood, poorly feigning shock. The count was seething with rage, most likely, and Enric wondered what precautions Divstan had taken to ensure the attack couldn't be linked to him.

Baron Veldenthane put his arms around his wife protectively, and then Azhlyn, as she ran in tears to her uncle. As the guards dragged away the assassin, the baron met eyes with Enric and nodded. His gaze was somber, but grateful. Grateful enough, perhaps, to finally grant the illusive's dearest wish.

Enric's chest tightened. His plan was working.

H e slowly paced across his chambers later that night, replaying the events of the banquet. The attack, the brilliant defense. Surely, after five years of loyal service and a life saved, the baron would be receptive to Enric's pledge for Azhlyn's hand. Enric should have been ecstatic. Instead he wanted to throw up.

Who had he become to have executed such a risky plan? What if the assassin had succeeded? What if he hadn't caught the illusion fast enough?

He conceded that it had been a well-calculated risk. Enric could detect the most complex of illusions, by the most talented of illusives, and Count Divstan's illusive was weaker than most. That had been part of the reason Enric chose the count in the first place. That, and Divstan's well-known hatred of the baron. Plaguing Divstan with expertly concocted illusions— spies reporting intrusions by Veldenthane onto the count's lands, as well as plans to discredit Divstan with the Queen—had been remarkably easy. The count, greedy murderous bastard that he was, had acted just as Enric anticipated.

But am I any better?

His question remained unanswered as a soft tap on his door was followed by its swift opening and even swifter closing. Like a blur, a vision in cream linen and beribboned hair, Azhlyn stood before him.

Enric gaped. Any words he could think to muster turned to sap in his throat.

She smiled at his obvious surprise. "Usually you look more pleased to see me."

Enric looked to the closed door and back, imagining servants on the other side with their ears pressed against the wood. Or worse, her uncle. "You can't . . . I mean, at this hour, to be in my room . . .," he started, unsure. Illusives were commonly thought too valuable to be put to death, but Azhlyn *was* the only daughter of the baron's late, beloved brother.

She laughed and made a dismissive gesture. "Don't worry so, it makes you twitch. I won't be long. And I promise to be utterly decorous the entire time." Tiny dimples winked at him from under a spread of freckles.

Enric was unmanned, as always, by that smile. "Of course, Azhlyn, I would never think otherwise." His most secret dreams, on the other hand . . .

Her dark eyes took in the room as she sat down on the end of his bed. While she looked away, he illusioned himself a bit— adding a touch more bulk to his slight frame, darkening his too-red hair just a shade. Nothing drastic. Azhlyn arrived at Grimweth three years ago, and by this time certainly knew what he looked like, even if she had barely sent a glance in his direction for the better part of those years. Something had changed, though, these past few months. She noticed him, smiled at him, spoke to him as if he mattered.

Enric swallowed hard and pulled out a chair from the desk to be his own seat. The flames burning in the hearth wavered Azhlyn's shadow across his bed. Her small fingers picked at a thread on her nightdress.

"You were incredible at the banquet," she said. "Saving my uncle's life like that. You have to know how grateful we all are. How grateful *I* am."

He had never before realized how sour the taste of guilt could be. "I'm glad he was unharmed," he said. How true that was. Baron Veldenthane had always been a kind man and a good employer, even if his barony was primarily composed of low marsh.

"Well, if I can't tempt you to brag about your heroism, I know you won't be able to resist when I tell you how realistic your illusion was." She shuddered lightly. "The dragon was terrifying. I'll be sure to blame you for any nightmares I have as a result."

Enric grinned despite himself. "It *was* realistic, wasn't it? I've been working on it for months, trying to get the details right." And worth every moment of his free time, though by the fatigue he felt weighing down his very bones, it had taken more out of him than expected. Many of his illusions had been, lately. Still, he was right to be proud. An illusion that size, that complex, with only the tiniest of ripples. He doubted the other illusive had even been able to find it.

Azhlyn's lips pursed. "Can you do one for me before I leave? Anything you want. I miss having my own personal illusions."

Enric's heart drummed faster. Several months

had passed since she had fallen ill and he had gone to her bedside daily to keep up her spirits with conjurations until her health returned. He had been so busy of late preparing the banquet illusion, not to mention setting up Count Divstan. But that wasn't all that kept him away. His infatuation had grown too strong, too all-consuming. He knew if the baron denied his pledge, if Azhlyn was betrothed to another, Enric would be destroyed. Being in her presence while everything hung so precariously in the balance was often more than he could bear.

But she missed him.

"Yes, of course." He barely had to concentrate before a flurry of color exploded before their eyes, along with the rustle of hundreds of wings. Butterflies, in a riot of vibrant hues that contrasted sharply with the gray stone and dark wood of Enric's room. Azhlyn gasped as they spread out across the small room, beating their wings against the ceiling and frosted window.

One landed on her open palm, glints of ruby and amethyst sparkling on fanned wings. She touched it gently, as if afraid the illusion might shatter with the slightest breath. It wouldn't, of course. The butterfly was small, and easily made tangible for a brief time. Enric could see the ripple, the faintest haze of unreality, but the effect was unavoidable. Every illusion had a ripple, no matter how simple or complex.

A stream began burbling past her feet, winding its way across the room. The water churned lightly, shimmering with the gold flecks of summertime. Azhlyn watched with her lip held between her teeth, even as her cheeks tugged at a smile. Enric felt his own smile, natural in a way he rarely felt, as he saw her happiness. She didn't try to touch the water, which was just as well. Making the stream feel real would take intense concentration, a focus Enric wasn't sure he could maintain while she stood so near him.

Her eyes tore away from the illusions and, through a riot of beating color, met his. She stepped across the stream, not looking down to notice the water form gentle swirls around her doe-skin slippers. All at once, she was before him, beside him, everywhere in the air around him. Her eyes closed. Enric felt her mouth against his, her soft lips tasting of spiced cider. His hand quivered in her chestnut hair and the scent of sandalwood filled his nose.

She pulled away. Butterflies winked in and out of existence like stars. With a blush and a demure tilt of her head, she said, "Thank you, Enric. I've never seen the like."

Then she was gone. The door closed behind her while Enric stood dazed inside a room returned to stone and wooden emptiness.

T he dream Enric had that night was surprisingly disturbing, given the achingly exquisite memory he clung to as he drifted into sleep. Once asleep, he no longer saw Azhlyn's freckled blush or felt her hair between his fingers. Instead he saw himself standing under a willow tree in the dark of night, long strands of leaves hanging around him. Sweat beaded across his brow. Tears trailed down his cheeks and he choked against a sob, even as he broke into the hard earth with a shovel. A long, enshrouded bundle lay against the escaped roots of the tree. The leaves rustled loud enough to block the sound of the shovel overturning dirt.

Enric felt a sharp sting on his cheek that pulled him into consciousness.

The loud rustling wasn't leaves at all, but rather the beating of hundreds of wings, frantic shadows of movement in his dark room. Butterflies swarmed over his bed, diving onto him and lighting as quickly away. Wherever they touched skin, Enric felt the searing pain of a knife-cut, and he cursed as he flailed his arms to keep them from his face.

A burning pain slashed across his eyebrow and thick blood dripped into his left eye. He cried out, but they filled his mouth, gagging him and biting savagely across his tongue.

One thought clung to his fear-addled mind as he spat furiously. *This has to be an illusion.* He grabbed one by its wings, gritted his teeth against the pain lancing through his hand, and tried to focus. He could find no ripple, but the pain and dark and constant flurry around him would have made seeing that impossible. He reached out to grab the illusion, sought to attach his mind to it like a savage dog, and yanked hard at the very fabric of it. Nothing happened.

They were real.

Another succession of stings against his hand, and Enric released the butterfly. He leapt from the bed and reached the door, but stopped. He couldn't let them into the rest of the castle. Not where Azhlyn slept. He felt rivulets of blood seep down his neck from hair matted with winged attackers. The pain drove him to his knees onto a strip of moonlight across the floor.

A strip of moonlight. The window. Enric pulled himself up and ran to the meager light. Crystalline frost etched the edges of the glass. He fumbled around on his desktop, near-blinded from the swarm about his face and the hundred tiny stabs of pain, knocking over his inkwell and quill set before he reached the candlestick. The thick candle fell out, but all he needed was the heavy pewter base. He turned back to the window and smashed the base into the glass with every desperate bit of strength left in him. The glass shattered. Cold air stole his breath and numbed the cuts across his face.

Hundreds of wings sparkled in the moonlight as butterflies fled the room. Still more continued to sting his head, his hands, and Enric dropped the candle base and flung himself as much over the narrow windowsill as possible, shaking and frantically rubbing at his hair until the sound of beating wings no longer filled his ears.

When he convinced himself they were finally gone, he pulled his blood-smeared hands back from his head. One hand had a long shard of glass poking from it. Blood slicked his cheeks, his left eye still closed against the trickle running down from his eyebrow. His hands shook. His breath rattled as he drew in gulps of air.

What *was* that?

Had someone seen him with Azhlyn and turned his own illusion against him? Was Divstan taking revenge against Enric for the thwarted attack? He dismissed the thought out of hand. Divstan's illusive had been caught. Besides, no one had the kind of power it took to make an illusion so real, to make it cut into skin, drawing blood and causing such pain. Pain that still throbbed across his head and face and hands. Had it been an illusion, he should have been able to stop it, even distracted as he was.

Something else, then. Enric trembled in the cold. He imagined with horror the dragon he had conjured for the banquet coming to attack. *Impossible. That would be impossible.*

But so was this.

After a long while straining for any sound, he built the fire back up and set his thick blankets as close to the hearth as he dared. Blood smeared onto the blankets and across his pillow as he laid his matted hair upon it. He found again the heavy candlestick base and clutched it tightly, while the whistle of wind and the snap of the fire eventually lulled him back into sleep.

When he awoke to the gray light of morning, he wasn't sure whether to laugh or weep. Nothing hurt but his hand, cut by the broken window. He touched his head, his face, looked for the blood he remembered staining the blankets, but all were in perfect condition. The thin layer of frost blown into the room and his bleeding hand were the only testament to the terror of his memory.

He chose to laugh. The sound of it frightened him.

He told no one what had happened and decided not to mention the broken window. A cloak stuffed into the jagged crevice would suffice to keep the cold out until he could think of a plausible excuse that wouldn't throw aspersions on his sanity to the uncle of the woman he hoped to wed. Enric himself tried to disregard the whole thing, blame the incident on over-strong drink or the mental exhaustion of the dragon illusion, or even the heady emotions stirred by Azhlyn's kiss. It worked, somewhat.

The following evening Enric awoke from the same dream as before, his hands clenched as tightly as they had been around the smooth wood of the shovel handle. What he awoke to was a room rapidly filling with water. A stream, pouring from the crevices in the stone wall. He cried out as he jumped from the bed and his feet hit the water, cold as Huntress Lake after the year's first thaw.

Enric dashed to the door and swung it out, letting the water rush into the hallway. Gripping the illusion, tearing it from reality, was no use. As before, there was simply no illusion to hold onto. No ripple to be seen within the swirling current. He ran toward the servants' quarters for help, for confirmation, *anything*.

Yet when he returned with several bleary-eyed kitchen boys, no trace of any water remained on the floor, no sodden rugs or wet-darkened stone. The boys looked at him dubiously and backed away. The next day the servants refused to meet his eyes, becoming fastidiously occupied with their duties the moment he entered a room.

He didn't blame them.

Enric winced at every request for an illusion for the next several days, but conjured anyway. He had no sane explanation for the baron as to why he couldn't perform his duties as always. Even the fatigue he'd felt more often of late was no excuse for an illusive of his power. Days passed, however, and nothing unusual happened.

Not until the evening after he encountered Azhlyn in the hallway outside the baron's study. She was singing softly as she walked around the corner, the light timbre of her voice lovely despite pitching several notes too low. She startled upon seeing him. To cover any awkwardness, he conjured a rose, its petals yellow with a blush of pink that matched the flush of her cheeks. She thanked him with a coy smile and brushed his fingertips with her own as she walked past.

That night he awoke with the smell of rot and decay thick in his nose. He thought it merely the bizarre dream again until he saw the yellow roses, hundreds of them like a vast rug across the floor of his room. They were fully open in the moonlight, with petals of silk to the touch, but the smell was unbearable. Enric retched violently into his chamber pot and burrowed under his blanket, shaking.

This could not go on. Enric needed answers. Early the next morning, he left the castle with a pack of food, warm clothing, and the horse the baron had given him last year. A hastily scribbled note lay on his bed, in a room that smelled neither of roses nor death. He hated abandoning the family, especially with his skills needed at the upcoming winter court, but he had no choice. He hoped the baron wouldn't reconsider the trust in him that Enric had risked so much to ensure. He hoped Azhlyn would understand. Most of all, he hoped answers did exist to find, and quickly, so he could return to his home and his love and the life he felt slipping through his grasp.

After a week of travelling, thankfully free of nightmares or inexplicable horrors, he arrived in Huth. The seaport city was not the largest in Kest-uruth, but the Guild presence here was strong. If there was any who could help him, Master Voss was the one.

Unfortunately, Voss had every reason to refuse to speak with him.

The city streets smelled of over-population and fish, a scent oddly comforting in its familiarity. He had lived in Huth for ten years after being taken in by the Guild when he was seven, much younger than they normally would take gifteds. But Enric had always been different from the others, isolated by his age and potential. The Guild had applauded his talent while eagerly anticipating the fat purses he would earn them.

He made his way to the Guild, not stopping for the calls of merchants greedily eyeing his stallion and thick ermine cloak. He stabled his horse at a local inn that catered to visiting illusives and followed the maze of streets until he reached the headquarters, a dilapidated old building that looked about to crumble at any moment. Not their best illusion, or most creative, but it did carry a convincing odor of must and rats.

The ripple was obvious, but hiding the building from illusives wasn't the intention. Enric carefully unraveled the illusion, his mind tugging at each thread precisely. This was nothing like ripping away the assassin's illusion at the banquet. This required patience and training. Specifically Guild training, which kept any renegades out.

As he worked, a fat orange cat slunk around his feet, sitting down to lick at one white paw. Enric pulled the last thread of the illusion free, and stared for a moment at the true face of the Guild headquarters. Pale peach stone cut at precise angles, with ivy climbing the walls and entwining above narrow arched windows. An iron-gated door, decorated in swirls that ended in points like knives, unlocked. Stately and imposing. Impeccable and unforgiving.

The sight of the ivy brought uncomfortably to mind the long strands of willow leaves from his nightmare. He drew in a deep, slightly ragged breath, and glanced down at the cat, unchanged since the first time he had seen him when Enric was seven years old. "Well, Fizel, I'm home."

Fizel mewed, unimpressed, and Enric went inside. As he closed the door, the illusion outside would be forming once again, as if he had never taken it apart.

He walked down the warm wooden hall, passing the student chambers and instruction rooms. Being here again was unsettling. Even though he had lived here for ten years, it had never felt like a home. A chattering group of young students passed him with curious stares. They only heightened his unease, reminding him that in all those years, he had never belonged to a group of friends. Never belonged to anything but his studies and potential.

Soon he stood before the door to Voss's study.

"Come in," came the gravelly voice in response to his knock. He pushed the door open. The old man still retained much of the black in his hair, what little he had left around the edges of a shiny bald pate. A thick volume lay open in front of him. Fizel dashed passed Enric and leapt onto his master's desk. The cat's edges rippled as it stretched languidly.

Enric shifted from one foot to the other uncertainly. Voss continued to stare down at the yellowed page for a bit longer.

"Is there something you need from . . .?" Voss's voice rumbled to a stop as his eyes lit on the young man standing in front of him. "Enric," he spat.

Enric swallowed. "There is something I need from you, Master. I know I have little right to ask, but . . . I need help."

"So you can continue to display your ingratitude? I'm not interested."

"My life doesn't belong to the Guild."

Voss snorted. "The Guild raised you, gave you the training to become great, and you were barely out the door before you shat on it. Now you want more? Is Baron Veldenthane not paying enough? Perhaps if you bothered to respond to the numerous attempts we made to hire you out to—"

"The baron pays me quite well, and the Guild is still receiving his dues. Just because you'd rather I reap you greater dues from richer nobles doesn't mean I have to oblige." Enric's voice was firm, although he did feel a bit like the spoiled child the Guild undoubtedly thought him to be. After all, he not only had refused every offer they had delivered for the past two years, but he had begun sending the missives back unopened. He hadn't even heard from them since harvest.

"I've put my neck in the noose for you time and again, assuring the Guild you aren't openly defying us, that you just need more time. All the while, I wonder why I bother, when you obviously care so little for those who gave you everything," Voss said.

Enric felt the words like a punch to the chest. His mentor had stood by him the whole time Enric had sworn off the Guild and every member of it as beneath him. He hadn't deserved that loyalty.

"I didn't know that. I should have assumed, when the Guild didn't come for me, but . . . I'm grateful. I truly am. I need your help, though. Not money, nothing like that. Advice. An answer, if there is one. *Please*."

The desperation in his voice appeared to catch Voss off-guard. The harsh wrinkles softened a touch, although the scowl remained. He motioned dismissively to a chair, which Enric took. Fizel mewed until Voss let the illusion crawl onto his lap, his stubby fingers stroking the orange fur.

Enric began his account, the words coming slow at first but gushing soon after as he told of his strange dreams and the illusions become real, become independent of his control, biting and freezing and sickening him. He told it all in exquisite detail, with two exceptions. He never mentioned his part in manipulating Count Divstan into the attack—a crime that would cost Enric much more than merely his position at Grimweth—or that it was only the illusions he created just for Azhlyn that returned to plague him. Voss might jump to conclusions about her that simply could not be true, conclusions that Enric refused to entertain. She was no illusive, and certainly not one holding that kind of power. Beyond that, he had little desire for Voss to discover the real reason Enric had thrown away a future with the Guild.

He finished his tale, gripping the sides of the chair to still the tremble in his hands. Voss exhaled slowly. His thick fingers scrubbed at a bushy gray-streaked eyebrow, a gesture Enric had seen many times before.

"You say they are real, yet they must be illusions."

"They *are* real. As real as you are now. At least, that's how they feel and smell and move. I know illusions, Master. Better than . . ." Enric trailed off, his head ducked.

"Better than me? Better than anyone in the Guild?

Your pig-headed cockiness is still intact, I see." Voss chuckled mirthlessly, stone scraping gravel.

"Do illusives sometimes . . . lose their concept of reality?"

Voss raised an eyebrow.

Enric swallowed. He decided to ask the real question. "Am I going mad?"

"I haven't seen you in five years, Enric. I am hardly qualified to judge."

Enric's hands tightened around the chair. "But you are. You know me. You practically raised me! And even more, you would know if this kind of thing ever happens to illusives."

"You have never been a typical illusive." Voss frowned thoughtfully. He held up a hand to forestall Enric. "However, there is one thing I do believe. Sometimes we make real what we need to be real."

"Why would I need butterflies to attack me or roses that smell of decaying flesh? There's no sense to it."

"I can't help you, I'm afraid. You've traveled all this way for nothing." Voss's gray eyes glinted. "Unless you wish to mend ties with the Guild. They could forgive, I'm sure, given formal contrition."

Enric's jaw clenched. With everything happening, the last thing he was concerned about was appeasing the Guild. He stood and began fastening his cloak about his shoulders.

"That's unfortunate," Voss said. "We have a promising battle position offered by General Intaro, but none currently free with the talent. Not after Count Divstan hired Kiruna."

"What?" Enric's fingers froze on the clasp.

"Kiruna? I'm sure you remember her. She had quite the gift herself. Divstan contracted her just last week."

Divstan hired Kiruna. She was good, almost as good as Enric, and the count would have paid handsomely for that kind of talent. Divstan didn't want to fail again. Enric's breath choked him. The winter court. Of course. The scene from his dream swam in his mind, of Enric turning over earth with a heavy shovel, sobbing above a shrouded body. Sobbing from grief? Or was it guilt?

He had to return. He had to stop Divstan.

"I'm sorry, Voss. I really am." He felt his mentor's piercing stare at his back as he all but ran down the hallway. He continued to feel it follow him the entire way back to Grimweth.

E nric's anxious eyes swept over the crowd in the grand hall. Dozens of people milled about, all garbed in the ragged wear of serfs. Several held foodstuffs or linens they would gift to the baron before presenting their case against their chicken-thieving neighbor or wheat-shorting baker. So far, nothing unusual. All looked genuinely disgruntled to be there, without a ripple to be seen.

He had ridden home with all possible speed, arriving late two evenings before winter court began. Veldenthane had been understandably upset about the unannounced disappearance, but, as Enric had returned by the crucial time, he had been mollified with Enric's solemn vow to never do such a thing again. That, along with a forfeiture of a month's pay, had settled things smoothly. Azhlyn, on the other hand, had been far angrier with him, although he could see relief in her eyes at his return. Enric hated having upset her, but there was something that thrilled him about it.

She worried about me. She worried about never seeing me again.

He would make it up to her. He would spend his whole life making it up to her, and gladly. But first, he had to see the baron safely through the winter court. And so he watched every detail, every flicker of movement. Not only in the items presented for debate, which was his usual function at such an event, but in every face. The guards were being especially watchful as well, given Enric's warning, but none were as vigilant as Enric.

If he dies, it will have been my fault. All of it.

Another of the seemingly endless arguments began before the baron. A woman pulled forward a scrawny goat, pointing a thin finger at the man she accused of poisoning the animal. A glance was all it took to determine that the goat wasn't illusioned to look thinner than it was. He nodded briefly at the baron, who proceeded to question the two.

The sensation of being watched pricked at Enric. He turned slightly to see Azhlyn's dark eyes regarding him from the side dais where she sat with her aunt. Enric smiled at her, although it likely came across as more tense than apologetic. Her eyelashes lowered briefly and she brought the tips of her fingers to her lips. Enric's pulse quickened, remembering. He turned his attention back to the crowd. He had to focus.

That was when he saw it. A young boy, whose hair might have been blonde under the crusty mud, sat holding a dead chicken that was undoubtedly to be a gift. Clearly agonized at being forced to sit still, he swung the chicken back and forth. The boy rippled—ever so slightly, barely discernable, but it was a ripple nonetheless.

"Guards!" Enric yelled, thrusting his hand out toward the boy, whose head jerked up in surprise. The guards jumped to attention, pushing people aside to reach where Enric pointed. The baron leapt to his feet, and several shrieks rang out in the hall. Enric found the illusion with his mind, although it was finely woven. He clenched his fist, and the boy shattered to the ground like crystal. More screams sounded and the guards stopped their approach. Nothing was there. No one stood behind the façade of the boy.

Enric's stomach dropped, just as he saw the glint from the corner of his eye. His head twisted to see the knife being drawn back, released. Released from a hand that had no ripple at all, that was nothing more than an assassin disguised in serf's clothing.

A wordless cry ripped from Enric's throat, and he threw himself at the baron, knocking Veldenthane to the floor. He felt something like a kick to his stomach and he went down, his head smashing against the baron's wooden chair before landing on the stone.

The room tilted unnaturally amidst the resulting chaos. Yells from the guardsmen mingled with the cries of the crowd. A woman screamed his name. Azhlyn. Her face appeared above his, tears streaked down her freckled cheeks. Her hand felt too warm on his arm.

The baron's face, brow creased above his brown eyes, was also above him. "Hold together, now," Veldenthane said. His voice held a hint of foolish self-awareness, like one talking to a gravestone.

Enric coughed, his whole body heaving with the motion. He felt the pain in his gut for the first time, felt the slick wetness on the hands he had wrapped around the protruding dagger.

"Enric, Enric," Azhlyn wept. A tear struck his cheek and burned like fire. "My love," she murmured. Her aunt wrapped an arm around the girl's shoulders, held her tightly. Enric ached to be able to do the same, but he couldn't seem to move more than his hands. He raised one to stroke her face, but the smear of too-bright blood covering his fingers stopped him.

My love.

"Azhlyn," he said. The room had dimmed slightly; her dark eyes were absorbing all the light. "Azhlyn, I wish . . ." He coughed again, choking. Her aunt gasped suddenly, pulling her arm back as if it had been stung. Enric didn't know why, didn't care. All that mattered was that the baron was safe, and that Azhlyn loved . . .

Enric blinked, stunned. He stared at Azhlyn, the center of the chaos swirling about the edges of his perception. Stared at her in total incomprehension.

She rippled.

Faint at first, the ripple grew more and more pronounced by the second. The baroness stared at Azhlyn as well, not seeing the ripple as Enric did, but her expression of horror betrayed the truth. She couldn't feel her niece anymore. There was only air.

"What? This can't . . . I don't . . .," Enric choked out. Despite the pain, tiredness began to descend upon him like heavy netting.

Azhlyn wiped at her tears with the back of her hand. "We can be together now, Enric. You can rest beside me, under the willow. You can finally be with me."

And he saw himself again, the long strands of willow leaves blowing against his grief-wracked face, turning over earth to bury the body lying still beside him. He felt the shovel in his hands, the warm summer night on his skin. More than a dream. A memory, hidden behind walls of unrealized grief.

"No, no, no," he moaned, as the walls crumbled, more memories flooding into his mind. He saw Azhlyn those many months ago, lying in bed from the terrible illness, her dark eyes unable to focus on the illusion he was conjuring. She shook from chills even as sweat beaded across her forehead. He reached for her hand, daring to presume himself a source of comfort, but she wrenched it away with a glare, weakly ordering him to leave. Her voice was all breath. Her eyes rolled back and her body seized before relaxing for the last time.

"I couldn't save her, I couldn't keep her here," he wept. "She needed to be here. I needed her to be here."

The memory was too much for him, too much pain to endure. Just as it had been that summer night.

We make real what we need to be real.

Azhlyn smiled, her face full of a love she had never felt for him in life. She flickered, disappeared for but an instant, as he lost more control with every fresh gush of blood. Her uncle recoiled from his niece, his mouth agape. The air around Enric filled with tiny black spots, dark stars in the gray light of the room.

Azhlyn's ripple distorted her face completely. Freckles danced across trembling cheeks. Chestnut hair wavered down contracting shoulders. She leaned down and touched her small pink lips against his once more. He felt nothing but air.

And then she was gone. Enric shook with his own soundless tears, his pain echoed in the sobs of the baroness, the horrified face of the baron. Enric licked his painfully dry lips. They tasted like blood and spiced cider, and he savored both as the netting of darkness pulled him downward.

The Faerie Journal

I had just finished checking my faerie garden when I heard the rattle and thump of my aunt's rusty van pulling into the driveway. Normally I'd hurry through the gate to the front yard to ask if she needed help with the groceries or whatever—Daddy was big on me repaying Aunt Lue's hospitality with "helpful hands"—but I hung back. Aunt Lue wasn't coming back from work or the store like usual. This time she'd brought my cousin home from war.

I eyed the bluebells as they trembled in a small gust of muggy Houston wind. Perhaps I should check that patch again. Papa Twilly always said faeries showed themselves more on important days, and today felt important. I parted the small petals carefully. This late in spring their blue was no longer as vibrant and pretty against the dark brown of my hands, the petals beginning to shrivel against the thickening heat of approaching summer.

Nothing. The flicker of a dragonfly, but no faeries.

I closed the journal that lay open beside me. Voices drifted faintly from the driveway: Aunt Lue, even Daddy. Which meant this was an important day for sure. I hadn't seen Daddy out of his bedroom in over three days. Another voice sounded, softer. Was that Janna? I didn't recognize my cousin's voice. I hadn't seen her since I was seven and we'd visited this very house for Christmas, back before Momma died. But that was five years ago. I wasn't a little kid anymore, and Janna probably wasn't the same teenage girl who'd put butterfly clips in my hair and taught me the words to a song that got me grounded when I sang it on Christmas Eve.

Back then I didn't even know about the faeries. It was only two years ago that Aunt Lue told me the stories of my grandfather, who everyone called Papa Twilly, and I'd started my very own faerie garden. Since then, I'd read every book I could find on the subject. That's how I knew the proper spelling for them—"faerie," not "fairy," which is a mistake a lot of books for little kids make. The serious ones, the ones that tell what kind of flowers and food attract them, the ones that have stories of people who've really seen them, always spell it right.

Daddy didn't believe faeries love cinnamon or are afraid of metal or that their leader is a majestic purple unicorn. Daddy didn't even believe faeries are real. Once I'd heard Daddy tell Aunt Lue that faeries were a white girl's foolishness. Which was ridiculous, even if the faerie books mostly did have stories about white girls. Papa Twilly saw faeries all the time, and he was a proud black man. He'd seen faeries in every color of the rainbow, and some besides. Many of them didn't have human skin at all, but were bark and leaves and moss with wings and limbs. So why would they care about human skin color?

"Lizzy!" Daddy called through the screen door. "You still out there? Luenna and Janna are here. Come in and see your cousin."

I brushed the loose dirt from my pants, though the knees on these jeans were so dirt-stained from days spent among my faerie garden that no amount of brushing or even washing would make them new again. I left the journal outside. On a day like today, I'd probably need to check again later.

Daddy squeezed my shoulder when I entered the kitchen. He was wearing the same clothes he'd been in last I'd seen him: his bathrobe over worn flannel pants. He didn't wear normal-people clothes much these days, but I guess that's not a problem if you never leave your room.

"Remember, Janna's been hurt, she's different. No staring," he said in a whisper.

"Yes, Daddy." I'd seen the pictures Aunt Lue had sent from the hospital.

But when I walked into the living room and actually saw my cousin in person, I ended up staring anyway. Janna wore a loose-fitting purple T-shirt with her high school track team logo on it and a pair of gray sweatpants that didn't manage to hide the fact that her left leg was missing, replaced by a fake metal leg that peeked out above her dirty white sneakers. She leaned on short black metal crutches that didn't look anything like the padded gray crutches I'd had the summer I broke my ankle. These didn't fit under her shoulders, but had handholds she gripped so tightly her knuckles paled.

Her face, though. The pictures had shown her

head wrapped in bandages, so I'd been—like some dumb kid scared by a movie—kind of expecting my cousin to arrive wrapped up and shambling like a mummy, and maybe even drooling.

The truth wasn't worse, but it wasn't better.

The left side of Janna's once pretty face looked like it had melted under the Afghanistan sun. Her left eye was totally closed and nearly skinned over, the corner of it tugged down in a constant tearless weep. Her lip, too. Her black hair, cut close to her head, didn't cover the ragged hole where her ear should have been. My skin felt itchy all over looking at her.

"Hi, Lizzy," she said. Her voice didn't sound like the Janna of the dirty songs of Christmas past. It was too deep, too slurred.

Daddy patted my back, and I remembered my manners. "Hi, Janna. I'm glad you're back."

The right side of her lip curled up into a kind of smile, though her right eye didn't smile with it. Maybe the shrapnel had hit that muscle, too. "Me, too, Sugarcube."

Her calling me the nickname she'd given me that Christmas after catching me eating sugar cubes straight from the dish should have made me feel more comfortable.

I smiled so she would think it did.

"Let's get you to your room," Aunt Lue said. "I've kept up those posters you liked, except for that god-awful Kane one."

"Kanye," Janna and I said at the same time.

My aunt shook her head. "Either way, Lizzy's sharing the room with you now, and her momma, bless her soul, would never forgive me for putting her little girl in the same room with *that*."

60

Janna slowly made her way to the bedroom. I didn't want to go in there, not yet, even though that's where all my books were. I went back to my faerie garden and peered into the patch of black-eyed Susans.

Daddy watched me through the screen door for a long time, but I pretended not to see him.

Papa Twilly's real name was Timothy William, which somehow became T. Willy, which eventually became just Twilly. Daddy's name was Timothy William, Jr., but everyone just called him Tim. I guess one Twilly's enough for any family.

I'd never met Papa Twilly, who'd died before I was born, but Aunt Lue told me all about him when Daddy and I moved in with her two years ago. Papa Twilly was a good man, fought in the Vietnam War and came home to a job working in plastics manufacturing. He married his high school girlfriend, my Nana Relia, and had four kids—Daddy and Aunt Lue and a set of twins who died soon after they were born. He also claimed his life was guided by faeries. "Life isn't easy, Luenna," he told my aunt one day after the twins died, "but my little friends are here, and we'll be okay."

Aunt Lue said he didn't tell many people about the faeries, because everyone he told thought he was crazy. Papa Twilly kept a journal, though, full of stories and descriptions and drawings of the faeries. Aunt Lue gave it to me a few months after I moved in, when I'd come home crying one day because the kids at school called me Orca. Even then I knew she didn't believe Papa Twilly's stories, especially since the Bible doesn't say anything about faeries. She just wanted to give me something so I'd forget about school and the whale sounds kids made when I walked by.

But when I read Papa Twilly's journal, I knew it was more than just stories. I knew the faeries were out there, and that one day I'd see them too. I just had to try hard enough, make them know I was here, waiting for them. The rest of the world may not believe in them, but I would believe hard enough to make up for everyone else.

A week after Janna's return, I sat in a patch of grass damp from the sprinkler Aunt Lue had turned on that morning. I looked back and forth between Papa Twilly's journal and one of my favorite serious faerie books. This book said faeries hated unnatural smells, perfumes and such, but Papa Twilly said a couple of his little friends used to only come out when he'd douse himself in Brut cologne. They'd perch on his shoulder like birds and whisper secrets of the forest into his ears.

Aunt Lue wouldn't buy me any Brut, so I'd snuck into her room after she left for work and sprayed on some of her drugstore perfume, coughing at the strong blast. It smelled flowery and not at the same time, like gardenia and roses rubbed with old pennies. Then I sat in front of the ring of stones I'd made for the faeries. Inside the ring were little bathroom paper cups filled with cinnamon and honey.

No faeries yet. I didn't blame them. I wrinkled my nose, still smelling the perfume on me even after a half hour outside.

The screen door banged shut behind me. Janna came out, using her crutches slowly on the steps down. She eased herself into the white plastic chair that was the only one left of the set of four Aunt Lue used to have out on the deck.

Though we shared a room, Janna and I hadn't talked much. She'd be sleeping when I went to school, and sometimes still be sleeping when I'd come home. Sometimes she'd just be sitting on the bed, staring out the window, tapping her fingers on her leg like there was an invisible keyboard. I'd started leaving my books out in the living room, so I wouldn't have to go into the bedroom very much.

Between Janna and Daddy spending all their days locked away, the house was very quiet until my aunt got home. I didn't mind. I was used to it by now.

"Mom says you're looking for fairies." The way Janna said it, I knew she wasn't spelling it right in her mind.

"Yes," I said, cautiously. I didn't know Janna's opinion on Papa Twilly.

"Found any yet?"

I looked down at Papa Twilly's journal, pages and pages of drawings and experiences. My notebook had pages and pages, too, but only of failed attempts. "Not yet."

She nodded, as if that confirmed something. "Did you take a bath in Mom's perfume? Maybe that's scaring them away." The side of her lip curled up like it had that first day. I was used to her new face now, but the difference between the two sides—one pretty and smooth, the other melted and scarred—still made my stomach a little floppy. Like my cousin was half herself and half someone else and neither version made a full person.

The smile on her face slipped when she caught me staring. I looked away guiltily and wiped sweat from my forehead. There wasn't much wind today, not that wind helped any this time of year. It just blew the heavy heat around. A fat bee buzzed near my ear, but I didn't bat it away. One of my books said bees were faerie scouts. Papa Twilly never mentioned bees, but who knows?

"How's school?" Janna asked. "Mom said you had a hard time when you first moved here."

"It's better," I said, though that wasn't really true. The kids didn't call me Orca anymore, but since I'd gotten boobs before any of the other girls, they started calling me Jugs and the boys laughed and tried to grab my chest in the hallway. But if my teachers couldn't stop it from happening, what was the point of telling anyone else? Daddy and Aunt Lue and Janna all had their own problems.

More silence, except for the twitter of a bird and the distant hum of freeway traffic two streets over.

"You can ask me, you know. About the war. About my face or my leg."

I looked back at Janna. "You want me to?"

She shrugged. "Better than no one talking about it all."

That made sense, I supposed. "Aunt Lue said you were driving a truck and a bomb exploded."

Janna let out a laugh, though it sounded more like a hiss. "I guess you know it all already, then."

"Does it hurt?"

"I take lots of pills. It's not so bad now."

I thought of Daddy since Momma died in the car accident, closed off in his room almost all the time. Writing his next book, he said, but he hadn't needed to be alone so much to write the first three. I wished there were pills that took away the pain of losing people like there were for losing legs. I wished even more that the faeries would come.

Janna watched me expectantly, a kind of challenge in her good eye.

I sucked in my lip, thinking. "Did you ever see someone die?"

She blinked, staring back at me, and for a minute I thought I'd failed at some test I didn't even know I was taking. Then, softly, "Yeah. Lots of people. My friends."

In Papa Twilly's journal, he talked about the Vietnam War. The faeries came to him there, too, though they weren't the same ones he knew from Texas. They were creatures of reeds and water, with wings of palm fronds and bodies slim as blades of grass. They'd whisper to him in a language he didn't understand and watch over him when he slept. He'd see them flutter over the bodies of the dead no matter what country they were from, saying good-bye to friends who'd never even known they were there.

I wondered what the faeries in Afghanistan looked like.

Janna must have gotten bored waiting for me to ask more questions, because she kept talking all on her own. "We were doing a supply run when we hit a land mine. When *I* hit a land mine. Then they attacked, pinning us down. Carter, Brooks, the LT, Rice, and Millaney—all of them but me died. Well," she said, barking out another of those not-laughs, "Rice is still alive, but he's worse off than me. He's a vegetable, pretty much. They'll pull the plug on him eventually. Probably better that way."

Didn't sound better to me. I turned back to the ring of stones. A roly-poly crawling around the base of the cup of honey curled into a ball when I touched it.

"You know Papa Twilly was totally bat-shit, right?"

Janna said, sounding angry all of a sudden. "Mom told me all those stories when I was a kid, too, and I even believed them for awhile. But mental illness runs in our family. Papa's mother went to a sanitarium and her sister killed herself. Even your daddy . . ." She trailed off, then shook her head.

"Daddy's not crazy. He's working on his book!" I yelled. Warm liquid spilled onto my fist, and I saw I had crushed the tiny cup of honey. I drew in a shaky breath. Best manners. Anger scared faeries. "And Papa Twilly wasn't crazy, either. The faeries are out there."

"Then why haven't you seen them?"

"Go away, Janna." I carefully set down the crushed cup, my fingers sticking together at the knuckles. Maybe the faeries didn't like DollarCo store-brand honey. I should ask Aunt Lue to buy a different kind.

I didn't look back as the plastic chair scuffled in the dirt as she got up, or as the crutches creaked and her pretend foot dragged across the ground. Then the sounds of her walking stopped.

"I remembered those stories after the bomb hit," she said. "There was all this movement and heat and pain, but no noise at all. And walking through it all I saw a giant purple unicorn, coming right up to me. Had the horn and everything. It watched me and I watched it. Then the noise came back and all the screaming and the gunfire, and the unicorn was gone."

My anger disappeared, replaced by pure shock. "You saw the purple unicorn? That's . . . that's . . ." I was going to say "impossible," because even Papa Twilly had never seen the purple unicorn that ruled over all the faeries. But if the faeries were real, that meant the unicorn was, too. Joy and envy pulled my thoughts in different directions like kids at tug-of-war.

"There was no purple unicorn," Janna said quickly. "The therapist said your brain does strange things in situations like that. It's like a coping mechanism or something."

But I didn't care what some therapist who'd probably never even read any serious faerie books thought.

"Maybe the unicorn saved you," I said.

Janna blinked her good eye, once, twice. "Maybe it shouldn't have."

Without another word, she went into the house, the screen door slamming shut behind her.

I spent days poring over every reference to the violet unicorn, ruler of faeries the world over, in Papa Twilly's journal. There wasn't much, really, since he'd never seen so much as a mystical hoofprint, but he'd drawn a picture based on what the faeries described to him. I traced that picture with my finger until I worried I'd rub the old ink right off.

I was happy the unicorn saved my cousin. But it chewed at me, deep in my gut. Why her? Why, when she didn't even believe, would she see the most rare of all the magical creatures?

Why couldn't I?

"Hey, Jugs," called a boy biking past with his friends on the way home from school. The boys pulled their bikes around to block me on the sidewalk.

My heart hammered in my chest. There was only

a week left of school. Why wouldn't they just leave me alone? My hands tightened around Papa Twilly's journal, palms sweating into the black leather.

"Do a dance for us, Jugs. Shake that fat ass," another of the boys said. His name was Andre, and he was the biggest and meanest of them all.

"Leave me alone," I said, looking around for a way out. There were four of them, enough to surround me. A car drove past, but didn't stop.

"We'll let you past after we see those big ol' titties dance," said Andre's puny shadow, Tyler. He had a face like a ferret and smelled like one, too.

"Go away." I tried to keep my voice firm and normal, even as I clutched the journal in front of the jugs they wanted so badly to see. I read once that bullies respond to direct statements said without emotion. That they only wanted a reaction and if you didn't give it to them, they'd leave you alone.

Maybe these bullies hadn't read that article.

Andre grabbed the journal from my sweat-slick hands and opened it.

"Stop it!" I cried, jumping at him to get it back, but Javier, the boy who'd first spoken, shoved me to the ground.

"Shit," Andre said, laughing. "There's like fairies and shit in here. Juggies likes that Barbie Snowflake stuff."

Tyler snickered.

Tears pricked at my eyes, and my knees stung from scraping against the sidewalk. "I'll scream! I'll scream and scream and you'll go to juvie where you belong if you don't give me back my book and leave me alone!"

But fear rooted me to the sidewalk, to the pebbles digging into my skin.

"Maybe Jugs will dance to get her book back," Andre said.

The fourth boy, Leon, turned from watching the far intersection. "The bus will be here soon. We'd better go." He lifted the front wheel of his bike from the ground a couple times. Nervously.

Hope flowered in me. The next bus stop was close by. If I screamed, surely someone would chase them away.

Andre flipped him off. "Dance for your book, Jugs." He ripped a page from the journal, and the sound was like my chest being torn open.

"No!" I shrieked, stumbling up to grab at Papa's journal.

"That's it," he laughed, ripping another page, crumbling it in his fist. I saw a flash of color, greens and browns and metal gray. The self-portrait of Papa in his war fatigues.

I rushed at Andre, intending to use every ounce of my body and my rage to knock him down, to shove his face into the pebbles, but Javier dropped his bike and grabbed me, followed right behind by Tyler. His stick arms were stronger than they seemed. I howled as Andre ripped another page free, making another crumpled ball of Papa Twilly's words and pictures.

"Andre . . ." Leon warned. The blue city bus had stopped two streets down. Still too far away.

What if the bus didn't stop here? What if it did and no one who got off helped me?

Why were the faeries letting this happen?

I struggled and kicked and even tried to bite, but the boys swore and laughed and pinned my arms so far back I thought my shoulders might break.

Andre ripped and ripped, page after page, tossing

the crumpled balls into the street, then with one final tear and crumple, he tossed the journal onto the sidewalk. He stepped up to me, avoiding my flailing kick, and brought his nasty face within inches of mine.

"Thanks for the show, Jugs," he said. His breath smelled of Doritos and root beer.

He took the last ball of wadded-up pages and stuffed it down my shirt. Then, with a final laugh, he gestured and the boys shoved me back onto the sidewalk. The four of them were halfway down the street on their bikes by the time the bus drove past.

It didn't stop. I watched the pages of Papa Twilly's journal bounce around the street in its wake.

When I got home, I had already wiped the tears from my face on my shirt. Aunt Lue would ask questions I didn't want to answer. The remainder of Papa Twilly's journal, along with the balled-up pages I'd gathered from the street and from my shirt, was in my backpack. I couldn't stand to look at it, to discover which pages would always carry the marks of what Andre had done, no matter how much I re-taped and smoothed.

To my surprise, it wasn't my aunt who greeted me when I walked in the door, but Daddy. He sat in my aunt's ugly avocado-colored armchair.

"Hey, Lizzy." He didn't look at me as he spoke, just kept staring out the window.

I followed his gaze. Nothing was out there, just the small brick ranch houses across the street that all looked like Aunt Lue's.

"Hey, Daddy."

I dropped the backpack on the entryway tile with a thunk. Aunt Lue would have been all over me about leaving my things laying around where people could trip over them, but Daddy didn't so much as raise an eyebrow.

I started toward the kitchen for a snack, but paused after a few steps.

"Are you okay, Daddy?"

He turned and looked at me for the first time in days. I'd forgotten how handsome my daddy was. Even more so in person than on his book jackets. Momma used to say his smile could charm the quills from a porcupine. He hadn't smiled in so long, I couldn't remember if that was true.

"What happened to your knees?" he asked.

"I tripped on the sidewalk."

He stared at me for a bit, and I couldn't tell if his dark eyes read the lie on my face or not.

"My publisher dropped me," he said.

I blinked. "But the book you've been working on—"

"They don't want it."

I didn't know what to say. My knees still ached, and so did my shoulders and my right elbow, though I didn't remember hitting that. "Maybe another publisher will."

He turned to the window again. "It's not done. I've barely got three chapters."

My chest turned hollow. He'd already started the book when Momma died. Two years in his bedroom, two years with the door closed on me and everyone else, and he hadn't even been working on the book, not at all.

"I'm going to check my faerie garden," I mumbled.

I didn't want to go back outside, but I wanted to be inside with him even less.

"They're not there, Lizzy," he said with a sigh. "Papa Twilly was wrong. We don't all have little friends looking out for us."

I walked numbly to the backyard. Bees crawled over the cups of honey, and tiny red fire ants scurried around a new hill they'd opened near my ring of stones. The bluebells hung low in the afternoon heat, dead white petals dropped onto the dirt.

I knelt down on the ground and stared at the flowers, not even seeing them. I began to sob, giant, racking sobs that shook my too-big stomach and my too-big breasts.

No little friends came to comfort me. Daddy had been right all along.

School finally ended, and summer cast its muggy blanket over the world. I only went out into my faerie garden one time, when Aunt Lue asked me to pick up the little cups of cinnamon and honey after she saw a raccoon rooting around our backyard.

I threw them away and kicked the stones around until there was no trace of a ring left. Just rocks scattered in the dirt.

I kept indoors like Daddy, like Janna. Aunt Lue would come in the house and peek into our bedroom and see Janna lying in bed, sleeping as usual, and me sitting on my bed reading something that was not my faerie books. I'd picked up some manga from the library, which I liked. Manga didn't ever pretend to be real.

Aunt Lue would sometimes ask if we wanted to go to the park or the museum, though we always said no—or I always said no and Janna kept sleeping. Sometimes, my aunt wouldn't say anything at all. She would just smile in a way that wasn't really smiling, but sad.

One day, after bringing Janna home from physical therapy and helping her back into bed, Aunt Lue said she hadn't seen Papa Twilly's journal around in awhile.

"It's in my backpack," I said.

"Still?" Aunt Lue glanced to where my backpack slumped under my chair like a deflated balloon.

I shrugged. I didn't dare mention the torn and still-crumpled pages. Aunt Lue might know better than to believe in Papa Twilly's faeries, but he was still her daddy and she'd be mad that I'd let that happen to his journal.

"She's twelve years old, Mom," Janna said. "She's over the fairy thing." She swallowed two blue pills and rolled over.

Aunt Lue watched me expectantly, and I turned another page in my manga book. She didn't even bother fake-smiling this time. She just looked sad, though I didn't know why.

Hadn't they all wanted me to see the truth about the faeries? About Papa Twilly?

That night, I woke to a strange scratching noise. I peered around the dark room. Enough moonlight seeped through the one broken blind that I could see that Janna's bed was empty, her sheets tangled. Her prosthetic leg, usually propped up against the nightstand, was gone.

"Janna?" I called quietly. Had she gone to the bathroom? And if so, why would she put on her leg? She would use just her crutches for that.

The scratching sounded again, louder, with a hint of the squeal chalk sometimes made on a chalkboard. Or like branches against glass.

Only we didn't have any trees by our room.

My heart beating erratically in my chest, I padded over to the window and opened the blinds. At first all I saw was light, white and so bright it seemed the moon itself had fallen into our window-well. Then the light dimmed, drawing to a point, and I realized that the actual moon was a tiny crescent mostly hidden by clouds. All the light in the window had come from this one narrow point, this one slim, spiral horn that had been scratching at the glass.

And that horn was attached to the head of a horse. A horse standing outside my bedroom window, with a mane and body so gray that . . . No. Not gray. As the horse stepped back from the window, the light from its horn gently illuminated a coat that was deep violet. Flickers of shadows with the shape of flowers and insects darted around it, just outside the light.

The purple unicorn had come. The faeries had come.

I trembled, barely able to think or breathe. I didn't bother pinching myself. I didn't dream much, and never like this. This was real. It had to be real.

I pressed my fingers to the window, the glass cool from the constant blast of AC. The unicorn bobbed its head twice, pawing at the earth with a glimmering hoof. Then it turned to the right and walked out of view.

"No," I whispered, afraid to say anything louder, afraid the trailing light from that mystical horn would burst like a bubble and leave me back in my faerie-less life. "Come back. Please, come back."

The light began to fade. I scrambled past my bed, stubbing my toe on a stack of library books as I ran to the kitchen and from there into the backyard.

The unicorn stood there, glowing serenely in the night, perfectly still against the flurry of tiny wing beats on the very edge of the light. Under the gaze of those coffee-dark eyes, my heart filled my whole chest, the warmth of light and hope and giddy joy spreading all the way from my bare feet to my bed-mussed hair.

I wished Papa Twilly could see this.

I reached my hand out slowly, carefully, hoping against hope that one of the faeries would come sit on my fingers or whisper forest-secrets in my ears, but froze partway. The unicorn pawed the ground and snorted, as if distressed. As if . . .

And then I saw her. Janna, lying on her side on the dying grass, the plastic chair knocked over beside her. An empty pill bottle peeked out from her curled fingers, and another sat a foot or so from her, half-hidden in a dandelion patch. The pretty side of her face was turned up to the light, her good eye closed.

"Janna!" I shrieked. The rustle of wing beats grew more frantic at my terror, and those at the outskirts of the unicorn's light fled.

I rolled her over, shook her shoulders. "Janna! Janna, wake up!" Her skinny body felt as heavy as the giant sacks of flour Aunt Lue got from Dol-larCo. Her head bobbed on her neck.

"Help her!" I cried, turning to the unicorn. "Please help . . ."

The unicorn was gone. The faeries were gone. The only light shining on Janna's face came from the back porch bulb.

I blinked, stupidly, then gathered Janna as close to me as I could. "Daddy! Aunt Lue! Help! Help!"

I screamed until the screen door banged open and Aunt Lue ran out in her nightgown and wailed and Daddy followed in his bathrobe and flannel pants and called 911. Then I held Janna until the ambulance came, and they pulled her from my arms and whisked her away.

I didn't go to sleep even after Daddy and I returned from the hospital. I pulled Papa Twilly's journal out of my backpack. I stroked the soft, worn leather of the cover and ran my fingernail over the ragged edges of ripped pages. Then I set to work with the crumpled balls of paper I'd managed to collect, smoothing out each one as gently and lovingly as if I'd been running my hand over the gleaming coat of the purple unicorn.

I didn't hear Daddy come in at first, but I did smell the hot chocolate. He set a steaming mug on the desk in front of me.

"She's going to be okay, they said. You found her in time."

I nodded. I already knew this. I'd been there when the doctors told him and Aunt Lue, and he'd said it at least twice in the car. Maybe he needed to keep saying it to believe it.

He sat on my bed, staring at the mug in his own hand. He lifted it as if to drink, but then lowered it again. "Your aunt, she knew Janna wasn't doing well. But she didn't know . . . I mean, none of us knew how bad it was."

I paused in my paper smoothing. This page

talked about how when Papa Twilly's babies died, the faeries wove a beautiful wreath of Texas prickly poppy and starlight for the gravestone.

"You're a hero, Lizzy," Daddy said. "She's alive because of you."

"She's alive because of the purple unicorn. And the faeries. They probably told the unicorn what was happening."

Daddy took a drink then, a long one even though it probably burned his tongue. He set the mug down on the carpet and leaned forward so his elbows rested on his knees. He looked me in the eye, really looked at me, and I was reminded of the unicorn's eyes, dark and mysterious and full of a kind of love too deep to understand.

"I'm sorry, baby. I'm so . . ." His voice broke, and he looked away for a second and then back. Red rimmed the edges of his eyes. "I'm so sorry. I've been a terrible father. I've been so lost since your momma died. And I've shut you out. I can't lose you, too, baby girl. I won't."

My throat felt thick, tight. I wanted to run away and I wanted to bury myself in his strong arms all at the same time, and so I didn't move at all.

He took my hand and enfolded it in his own, warmed by the hot mug and soft like bluebell petals. "I know I need to earn back being your daddy. And I will. I will be there for you from now on. The thing is, I don't know if I can believe in faeries or unicorns. But I believe in you. I believe in us."

I didn't forgive him, not then. Not yet. But he was my daddy. I dove into his arms and let him hold me. I breathed in the smell of him, like old books and coffee, a scent I'd loved and forgotten. I sobbed into his chest, releasing the pain of the bullies at school, the fear of seeing Janna's body on the ground, the ache that had never left since Momma died. It hurt and felt good, all at once.

I knew then that it didn't matter if he didn't believe in the little friends. It didn't even matter if I ever saw them again. They were there.

And we'd be okay.

Hotel of the Damned

W hen the bell rang on the makeshift front desk in the study, I was folding laundry and not particularly in the mood to play hostess to the dead. But if there's one thing I'd learned since the lost souls started showing up, it's that ignoring them doesn't do a speck of good. Eventually I started charging. You'd be surprised at how creative ghosts can be at coming up with money, especially the type we get around here.

I walked into the study and set the laundry basket next to the bars of soap I'd bought earlier that day. Ghosts don't use soap, but my husband and I do, and besides, the guests seem to appreciate it when I put a new bar in the bathroom. They like the lavender smell best when it's just out of the wrapper.

I barely glanced at the tall figure standing at the desk as I sat down and opened the check-in form on my computer. I already had a new one ready.

Room One's former occupant, a skinny rock band bassist who the magazines said died of a drug overdose, checked out yesterday. And every time we had a room available, a new guest always showed up within a day or two, like clockwork. It's not like we put up an ad or anything, but somehow it always happened. One room, one guest. I'm thinking the Marriott would kill for that kind of guarantee.

"You're needing a room, I take it?" I used to work harder on the niceties, but playing chipper receptionist lost its charm as quickly as washing ghost imprints out of bed sheets.

"Yes, ma'am. Please," the man said, and his voice was soft and deep. Polite. I liked that. I checked a box to remind myself to give him his own scented bar of soap, on the house.

"Just so you know, we don't have HBO or any of those premium channels. I don't care for the language they use."

"That's just fine, ma'am."

"And how did you hear about us?" It was a useless question, because none of them ever knew exactly how they had come to my house. I always asked anyway, though, because maybe one day I'd get a real explanation for how our home became a Motel 6 for the dead. Our house wasn't some old slavery-era mansion where you'd expect to find hordes of wandering spirits swapping tales of injustice. Just a red brick two-story in the Kansas City suburbs, three blocks from a gas station and a Kaptain Kluck's Chicken.

"This is where they all come, isn't it?" He cleared his throat. "I thought I should finally join them."

That's when I looked up and really saw him for the first time. He was taller than average, his extremely broad shoulders cloaked in a long wool trench coat as rumpled as his lined, kindly face. Like all the others, his overall aspect was grayish and slightly transparent. Unlike them, his expression didn't speak of confusion or sorrow or fear. All I saw in those dark, shadowed eyes was resignation.

Strangest of all, a pale glow radiated from him, flickering like a dying fluorescent bulb. I hadn't ever seen that before.

"Excuse me?" I said.

"You do have a room available, don't you, ma'am?"

"Um, yes. Of course. Guest room one." I tried to recover without showing how unsettled I was. A manager of a hotel for the dead should be able to take a little flickering light in stride. "I think you'll like it. It looks out over the garden, and my husband's finally gotten the roses to bloom this year."

"Perfect."

"There's an agreement I'll need you to sign, of course." I pulled out a standard contract, beginning to feel back in my element. "Payment is due at the end of each week, or on the morning you choose to check out, whichever comes sooner, and you'll find a list of establishment rules. Mostly they involve keeping the volume on the T.V. down, staying out of my bedroom, and not corporeally inhabiting any living being on the premises, including my cat." *That* had been an unpleasant addition to have to make.

The man smiled, though there was little humor in it. "Sounds reasonable to me."

"Dinner is at six, and guests are allowed to come to the dining room and mingle." The mingling part never seemed to take, since the folks I got here liked to keep to themselves, but they always came down anyway. Probably just to smell the food.

I finished with the standard warning. "If any guests break establishment rules or otherwise cause trouble, I'll send for my brother Tom. He's a priest." He also had the manners and mouth of a New York City cop, though I never mentioned that part. We'd only had to enforce this warning one time, and after a beat-down with the cross, a flask of holy water, and a variety of cuss words culled from second-rate film dialog, that particular spirit moved on of his own accord, apparently deciding hell would be preferable. No one since had risked it.

"All right." The man gave the contract a cursory glance, then picked up the nearby pen and signed. Unlike in the movies, ghosts are perfectly capable of manipulating objects when they want to, which was a relief to me when I started running this business. The last thing I wanted was to run between rooms constantly because my guests couldn't use a television remote.

He set down the pen, and his dark eyes swept over the clutter of St. Louis Cardinals memorabilia lining the shelves around the study. Rick, my husband, had been willing to go along with this hotel endeavor, but not at the cost of his Cardinals room.

"I'll show you to your room," I said, picking up the laundry basket and starting down the hall. I didn't hear him following me—you never do—but I knew he was there. I could feel something in the air, something different than the slight chill emanating from the usual guests. With him, the air wasn't warm or cold, but slightly charged, like towels fresh out of the dryer after I'd forgotten to put in the dryer sheet.

The guest in room three poked her head out

directly through the door as we approached, and I fought back a biting remark about manners. Passing through doors and walls wasn't in the contract, but most understood I didn't like it much. She was a large woman in a floral-print dress, and her face wore a permanent scowl. Some nights, though, I would hear her crying in her room and begging forgiveness from someone named Stanley, so I tried my best to be pleasant and hoped she would check out soon.

She wasn't scowling now. Her eyes widened in their fleshy pockets, and her mouth gaped a bit before she pulled her head back and disappeared into her bedroom.

"Here it is," I said, opening the door to the room at the far end of the hall. "Mr . . .?"

"Harper. Thaddeus Harper." He smiled again, and his teeth, all straight and even except for one crooked canine, flickered like the rest of him. It was hard to look directly at him for too long, like it might give me a headache.

"All right, Mr. Harper. I'm Carolyn, but everyone just calls me Carol."

He didn't respond as he followed me inside, just looked around the room, taking it all in—the faded blue paint on the walls, the multi-colored checked quilt and mismatched pillows on the bed, the cheap plywood dresser topped with a green vase I had picked up at a garage sale for fifty cents. I never was any kind of decorator, and normally it didn't bother me, but suddenly it did. I couldn't be in here anymore to see his disappointment.

"If you need anything—" I started.

"This room," he said, turning to face me. "Was it special to you?"

I blinked. Out of hundreds of guests, not one had

ever asked me that before. "Yes. A long time ago."

He arched a thick, ghostly eyebrow.

"It used to be my son's room," I said with a finality in my tone I usually saved for arguments with Rick. I turned away to leave the room, clutching the laundry basket tight enough to turn my knuckles white.

"Thank you, ma'am," Thaddeus Harper said. I didn't look back. At least, not until I was out in the hallway and had started to close the door behind me. Just before it closed, I saw that he had taken off his trench coat and was standing there in an equally rumpled business suit.

It turned out he wasn't so broad-shouldered, after all. But he did have wings.

My brother Tom, otherwise known as Father Hannigan to his suburban Kansas City flock, returned my urgent phone call later that night as I put the finishing touches on my chicken parmesan. I checked the clock as I put the chicken in – 5:37. Dinner would be late tonight, but the guests wouldn't care, since they didn't eat anyway. Rick, on the other hand, wouldn't be thrilled. He liked a well-ordered day, especially where his stomach was concerned.

But I couldn't put off talking to Tom.

"What do you know about angels?" I asked, skipping the usual pleasantries. I tried to keep my voice low, though I wasn't sure it mattered. Thaddeus might be able to read my mind, for all I knew.

"Angels? Plenty. Seraphim, Cherubim, Dominions. . . there's a whole mess of heavenly hosts up there. Why do you need to know?" I could hear

Tom chewing something, and I couldn't help but picture donuts.

"Because I think I have one staying here."

The chewing stopped. "That can't be right. Aren't your guests always, you know, damned?"

I sighed. Tom knew I didn't like that word, biblical though it may be.

"Fine," Tom said. "Headed to the eternal slammer. Is that better?"

"Worse, actually, but yes, that's what they've told me. The few that tell me anything, anyway." I poked my head into the hallway, but I didn't see any of them. I heard a gulping, sobbing sound that undoubtedly came from the woman in room three, but the rest were quiet tonight.

"An angel of God can't be damned. Their nature won't allow it."

I frowned, digging in the pantry for the box of penne noodles. "He had wings, Tom. What else could he be?"

Tom started chewing again, and I heard the rustle of paper. "Wings, huh? Could be one of the Devil's angels, I suppose, though I don't know why he'd hang around there. Not too much more trouble your guests can get into at this point. He's not causing you any grief, is he? Because if I need to come out again and bust some heads—"

"No, he's very polite. I don't get a bad feeling from him or anything, but I don't get a particularly good one, either. He just seems . . . tired."

"Maybe you're starting to get a better kind of clientele."

"I don't know. He said he wanted to 'join them.' Whatever that means."

"Look, I've got to get ready for tonight's mass.

But I'd like to see this guy for myself, especially if he is a real-life angel. That would be something, for sure."

"Yeah, it's something." I stirred the noodles into the boiling water. "You know I don't like surprises, Tom, and it took me long enough to get used to my house being a haunted rest-stop. Now I've got to deal with angels from who-knows-which side of the fence, and what's next? Demons? Because I swear, if anything comes in here with horns or a tail, I—"

The words cut off in my throat. Thaddeus Harper stood in the kitchen entrance, flickering eerily. His trench coat was back on.

"Carol?" Tom's voice sounded concerned. Fat lot of good concern would do with Tom and his holy water miles away if Thaddeus was something less than angelic after all.

I swallowed hard. "I have to go, Tom. I'll call you tomorrow." I hung the phone up before he could protest.

"Sorry, ma'am," Thaddeus said. "I just wanted to ask if you needed any help with supper."

I blinked. None of my otherworldly guests ever asked to help with anything, even in the days before I started charging them to stay. Heck, even Rick never did more than show up at the table and eat.

I looked around at the boiling pot of noodles, and the vegetables on the counter, waiting to be chopped for the salad. Nice though Thaddeus may seem, I wasn't ready to hand over any sharp knives quite yet. "You could set the table, if you'd like."

He nodded and continued watching me until I realized what he was waiting for.

"Oh, plates are in that cabinet there, above the toaster, and silverware is in the drawer by the fridge." It felt strange directing someone else around my kitchen, especially someone hiding a set of wings under a large trench coat, but I guess it wasn't the strangest thing I'd done since the guests started arriving.

He began pulling out the plates—white with an ugly 70's era brown pattern, a set that somehow managed to survive through nearly three decades, while that expensive set I bought from the department store was broken within two months. Of course, that was during the time I was teaching Shawn how to load the dishwasher.

The thought of Shawn dredged up the numbness, the tired ache always hovering behind the curtains of my life. Curtains I needed closed to function.

"You only need two," I said, my voice colder than intended. "For me and my husband. Unless . . . do angels eat food, Mr. Harper?"

"No, ma'am," he said, pleasant as could be. Catching him off-guard wasn't going to be so easy, it seemed. He took the two plates and the handful of silverware into the dining room. I frowned at my pasta. Maybe he *could* read my mind. Or maybe I had just been talking louder to Tom than I thought.

Movement caught my eye from the window above the kitchen sink. A raven sat there on the sill, its black feathers gleaming with an oily sheen. It cocked its head at me and stared.

That beady-eyed stare never failed to unsettle me. I'd been seeing the ravens more and more the last several years. Or maybe it was just the same one, over and over, drawn to the house inexplicably in the same way my guests were.

Too bad I couldn't charge birds the way I could

ghosts.

I rapped my knuckles against the window to scare the raven off, just as the front door opened and closed again harder than strictly necessary. This didn't bode well for Rick's attitude tonight. Seeing an angel sitting with us at supper probably wouldn't make it any better.

Rick entered the kitchen, his expression grim. He wore his usual work clothes, khakis and a black polo shirt with "Henderson Air-Conditioning" above the pocket. Unlike me, he still wore the same size he had twenty-five years ago when he was first hired. The lucky jerk had always been naturally thin, whereas my lifetime membership at Weight Watchers did about as much good as the treadmill gathering dust in the corner of guest room two. He gave me a quick, almost unnoticeable kiss on the forehead, a hold-over from the early years of our marriage. Only back then, it had been more than just habit. "Smells good."

"It's going to be awhile yet," I said. "Things came up."

"Figures." Rick tugged open the fridge and pulled out one of his non-alcoholic beers. He hated the taste of them, but he hated the thought of turning back into the man he had been after Shawn's death even more. And suggesting he switch to pop just made him ornery.

"There's a new guy. In room one." I tried to put some emphasis on this, but our days of reading each other's hidden meanings were as long gone as my natural hair color.

"Huh," Rick said, taking a swig of beer. He grimaced. "I'll go watch the pre-game. Give me a yell when dinner's ready."

"Sure thing." I probably should have asked him about work, since it was obvious the day hadn't been a great one, but it was hard to sympathize with air-conditioning-related problems when I dealt with the dead all day long.

A trail of ghostly figures passed by the kitchen door to the dining room. Six o'clock, right on time. Ghosts were nothing if not punctual. Rick looked down at his brown loafers, scrubbing self-consciously at his hair, which had thinned considerably in the last several years. He accepted the presence of the lost souls residing here, as the extra cash they brought in allowed him to expand his baseball memorabilia collection, but he still preferred to pretend they didn't exist. I wondered if he would be able to do so as easily under Thaddeus's steady, flickering gaze.

When they had passed, Rick hurried through the hallway. Our cat, Jinks, who was equally as unsettled by the spirits as Rick, darted after him from his hiding spot in the pantry.

"Is there anything else I can do?" asked Thaddeus from the direction of the dining room. Though he had stayed out of the kitchen while Rick was here, I knew he had heard everything. More than that, I knew somehow he had *seen* everything, even those things which weren't really visible.

"No," I said, pulling the pot off the stove. I didn't want his knowing gaze on me, or on my marriage, or my shabby, mismatched kitchenware. I didn't say anything more, and I felt the static-y presence of him leave the room as I finished chopping the vegetables.

When the chicken parmesan was finally done, and I had called Rick and Jinks away from their bonding time in front of ESPN, we settled down at the table.

Dinner together as a family was another habit we kept faithfully, even after our family of three became two, and then became two and a handful of ghosts. I'd read many an article in magazines about unconventional families, but I'm pretty sure we weren't what they had in mind.

We didn't say grace or anything unless Tom was over because it made the guests uncomfortable, and neither Rick nor I had been particularly religious even before we lost the one thing we had ever really thanked God for.

Rick dug into the dinner without saying a word, but I only took a few bites. I wondered how Rick could eat so calmly, not even noticing the new guest we had, the unsettling way he glowed and watched us. The ghosts at the table stared at the food on our plates, though I couldn't imagine they were actually hungry, being without stomachs and all. I had long since given up on trying to get a good conversation rolling at the dinner table, but something about the way Thaddeus sat across from me, his eyes not on the food, but instead taking in each ghostly face, then mine and Rick's—as if we were no different—made me long for distraction.

"So how is everyone enjoying their stay so far?" I asked, forcing myself to smile.

The guests looked up from the food, and I felt the cold stare of five sets of ghostly eyes. And one set of confused husband eyes. No one responded.

"Maybe we should get to know one another a bit," I continued. "Make dinner a bit more personable."

The ghosts didn't blink. I wasn't sure if they ever blinked. I tried never to look at them for very long. Thaddeus gave me a small, sad-looking smile. Rick just stared at me, his fork paused half-way to his mouth.

"You all know my husband Rick and I, of course. And our cat, Jinks. We've had him for twelve years, you know, but he still acts like a kitten sometimes, doesn't he, Rick?" My voice was bright enough to use as a flashlight.

Rick swallowed. "Uh, sure."

"He sure does," I said. I turned to the guest directly on my right, a short, balding man wearing a track suit. He'd only been here a week and might not realize how unusual dinner conversation among the dead was. "How about you, Mr . . . Kirman, is it? Can you tell us something about yourself?"

Mr. Kirman flinched. His eyes darted to his companions, then he nodded. A few wisps of ghostly pale hair on the sides of his head shook with the movement. "Yes, I, well, I have a daughter who lives in Pittsburgh, and three grandchildren." He paused. "Or, uh, I *had* a daughter and three grandchildren, I guess."

"How nice," I said, hoping to encourage more. *See, Thaddeus? I know how to make my ghosts feel at home. I just don't know why I'm suddenly trying to now.*

"You *had* them?" asked the scowling woman from room three. "Are they dead, too?"

Mr. Kirman shifted uncomfortably. "No, just me."

"Well, that's—" I started.

"What did you do to end up here?" The question came from the guest across from him, a man who looked to be in his thirties, with dark buzz-cut hair and round John Lennon-style glasses. He resided in one of the basement rooms, always paid a day early, and hadn't spoken a word in the three weeks he had lived here.

My mouth dropped open. "I don't think we—"

"I don't know," Mr. Kirman said with a shrug. "I cheated on my taxes once or twice."

"Taxes?" Lennon-glasses (whose name was Marco something or other) snorted, a sound I never thought I'd hear from a ghost at my dinner table. "You've got to be kidding."

Mrs. Li, a middle-aged Asian woman who occupied the other basement room, frowned at him. "You should not mock," she cautioned, in a tone that could chill a Yeti.

"I'm dead, aren't I? And I don't see any pearly gates in my future, so I doubt that taking a shot at Squirmin' Kirman here is going to make my situation any worse," Marco said.

"Worse?" My hackles shot up like Jinks's whenever the neighbor's greyhound raised a leg on our tree. "Excuse me, but I try hard to make things pleasant here. In fact, I just bought some more soap."

My assorted dinner companions didn't appear to notice my presence. Apparently once ghosts start unburdening, there's no stopping them.

"There are no pearly gates," Mrs. Li said with a sniff. "You believe in children's stories."

"Well, I think we know why you're here, honey," the woman in room three said. "God doesn't like atheists."

"I am Buddhist," Mrs. Li hissed.

"Same thing."

"It doesn't seem like God is happy with you either, lady," Marco pointed out with a smirk. "And neither is Stanley, whoever the hell he is."

The woman's mouth opened and closed, and I

swear I could see her cheeks flush, despite her being, well, transparent. "Don't you even speak his name!" she cried.

"Let's stop now," I cut in, looking around desperately. I didn't like confrontation, and I was especially wary about it around spirits. Who knew what they could do if they got upset enough? I noticed Jinks had wisely disappeared.

"Seriously, because we all want to know—did you kill him?" Marco asked, leaning forward, his eyebrows raised.

The woman—I couldn't remember what in the blazes her name was—seemed to fold inward, a vague outline of air deflating. She sat there, a large woman who looked suddenly small in grief. "I'm not talking about him with the likes of you," she mumbled.

"I just want to know if he's going to be showing up here anytime soon. Is that what you've been sticking around here for? To see if he's going to the same place you are?"

"Enough!" I jumped to my feet, knocking over my glass of Diet Coke in the process. Bubbly black liquid pooled around my plate and dripped onto the carpet. I felt hot tears prick at the corner of my eyes. "Well, then, look at this," was all I could say.

The guests fell silent, back like they were before I decided to play the happy hostess. Rick avoided my gaze, like he was embarrassed to look at me. "I'm going to catch the rest of the game," he said. He left with his plate and fake beer in hand.

I used my napkin to sop up some of the Coke on the table, but then I just sat back down, took a bite of rubbery chicken and ignored the dark stain still spreading across the tablecloth. Coke continued dripping onto the fifteen-year-old carpet, next to the red nail polish Shawn had spilled years ago, a stain that seemed to grow angrier with each cleaning.

I found myself glaring at Thaddeus, though in truth, he'd had nothing to do with tonight. His expression was blank. Flickering that maddening soft glow, but otherwise blank.

The silence stretched on, the ghosts back to watching the food disappear, bite by slow bite, from my plate, when Mr. Kirman let out a small, rueful sigh.

"I did spit on a homeless man once," he said. The others, with the exception of stone-faced Thaddeus, eyed him with mixed expressions of disgust.

I groaned, grabbed my plate and the wadded-up, Coke-soaked napkin, and left the table.

W hen the phone rang the next day, the pit in my stomach told me before I even answered that something had gone terribly wrong. Rick's car had been hit crossing an intersection. T-boned, the hospital nurse said. He was alive, she assured me, though he was in critical condition.

The hospital was familiar, from the time in Shawn's teen years when he suffered from asthma badly enough that he was checked in for pneumonia at least once a year. The long corridors smelled of antiseptic and desperation, and the floor was still that horrid, falsely cheerful teal color. I recognized some of the same motivational posters, and a few of the pastel-scrubbed nurses, though it had been long enough that they, too, looked more worn around the edges than before.

Rick wasn't awake when I came in. The doctor arrived in the room not long after I did, bearing the requisite clipboard and tightly sympathetic expression. She told me that he woke for short periods, but that the drug being pumped into his arm from one of several tubes kept him mostly asleep. Early scans had shown brain trauma, though the extent couldn't be determined. There was more to it, but all I saw was the man I had spent more than half my life with lying in the slim bed, pale and silent, trailing tubes and wires.

Tom arrived not long after I did, clutching a worn Bible in his large hands, and the little conversation we managed was in small whispered spurts. It was as if we were afraid that waking Rick would damage him further, even though all I wanted was for him to open his eyes and remind me to record the game.

He didn't.

After several hours, Tom offered to sit with him so I could run home and pack some things to stay overnight in the hospital. I figured I would check in quickly on the guests, none of whom I had heard a peep from since I had turned our dinner last night into a bad episode of Dr. Phil.

I didn't need to look very hard for them, as the whole ghostly lot of them were standing in my dining room, staring out the sliding glass door to the backyard. None of them even turned a head when I walked into the room. Through their mostly-transparent shapes, I could make out a figure near the large oak tree.

"What's going on?" My voice came out shriller than I'd expected. "What are you all doing?"

The heads turned to me simultaneously, in that creepy way they often had in acting as one.

95

"He left the house," Mrs. Li said.

Marco pointed his long thin arm toward the tree. "He's just been standing there. For, like, an hour."

I didn't have to ask who.

"What does he think he's doing?" I grumbled to myself. Mr. Kirman started to answer, but one look at my expression shut his mouth fast. I cleared my throat until the ghosts parted (because I sure as all that was holy was not going to walk *through* them), then slid open the door and stepped out into my yard.

I hadn't been out here in ages. Yard work had always been Rick's domain, and even more so since he had taken up gardening on the advice of his therapist. By now it felt so fully his own that I was like an intruder in his world of close-trimmed rose-bushes and thickets of untouched memories. We only had one big, ugly oak out back, and I could rarely bring myself to look at it.

Thaddeus stood under the oak tree, staring up into its branches, flickering just as he had inside the house. But now, outside, he wasn't wearing his trench coat, and his wings opened and closed slowly.

I glanced behind me, and saw the ghosts watching in mute fascination through the glass. They all left the house on occasion, usually right before they made their room payments (with what I could only hope was money acquired in a reasonably legal manner, though it's not like I pictured any of them working the late shift at Kaptain Kluck's). But never in their more solid, recognizable forms, and never in broad daylight. I have neighbors, after all. We may have privacy fences, but nosy Mrs. Fernstein next door was known to use a stepladder to spy on the progress of Rick's rose garden. The old bat would probably die of shock to see some strange man standing in my yard, let alone one that was dead and had wings.

"Mr. Harper," I said, sharply. "You can't be out here like this."

His wings folded stiffly against his back with the soft hiss of scissors closing. I had only seen his wings once before, through the crack of the door for that brief second, but they seemed different now. More solid, though the rest of him looked as ghostly as the guests pressing against my glass door.

"I am sorry about your husband," he said.

My frown deepened enough that I could practically feel it cutting lines into my face. "How did you know about Rick? I didn't tell any of you why I left."

He turned to face me. "We know things that others don't."

"We? Like 'we' my paying guests, or 'we' the hosts of heaven that have no understandable business here?"

"Do you wish for me to leave?"

Yes, I do, I almost said, but I bit the response back. He still hadn't done anything wrong, and I considered myself fairly open-minded. Not the type of person to throw out a guest based on a few wings or cryptic statements, no matter how much stress I was under. "I wish for you to come inside before Mrs. Fernstein sees you, and I get a very angry letter from the Homeowner's Association."

"I was listening to your son."

All those crazy things they say in books about how a character's blood froze, or their stomach dropped down into their knees and that sort of thing, all happened to me in the space of a second. I reached out for a patio chair to steady myself, to keep my legs from failing entirely. In the five years since the ghosts had started coming—heck, since Shawn's death a year before that—this had been my greatest fear and most impossible hope all in one. I couldn't breathe, but somehow the words came out anyway. "Shawn . . . he . . . he's here?"

If angels winced, I would say that was what crossed Thaddeus's face. "No, ma'am, not like you think. But I can hear him, the child he was that used to play in this yard. I can hear his laugh in the tree, and his footsteps on the grass."

My chest was heaving, disappointment and relief warring in me and spilling out as hot tears I furiously wiped away. "I am his mother. How can you hear things like that, but I don't?"

"You do," he said simply, and I knew it was true. I heard those things, and more, so much more, every night when I lay in bed and every morning before I opened my eyes. Still, he had no right to those sounds, this being I didn't know and couldn't begin to understand. "Not here, though," he continued, "because you block yourself from this place. From this tree. Why do you do that?" He cocked his head to the side, and I felt his desire to understand like a magnet, drawing my leaden words out before I even formed them in my mind.

My gaze rose to the wide-spread branches, despite myself. That blasted raven was up in one of them, and it cawed once before flying off. Goosebumps raised on my arms at the sound.

"Because whenever I look at it, I think of how he killed himself," I whispered. Shawn had hung himself in his apartment his sophomore year of college. I hadn't been the one to find his body hanging from a high ceiling beam in his room, feet dangling inches above a worn, balled-up Cardinals t-shirt and the prized baseball bat he'd hit the game-winning home run with, before the asthma got bad enough to keep him from playing. I hadn't seen his body there, and so maybe that was why I pictured it limp and cold, a dark silhouette swaying from the tree he used to play in when he was little and mine to protect.

"I've changed my mind," I said, trying to still the tremor in my hands. "I want you to leave, Mr. Harper. This is no place for angels. Or whatever you fancy yourself to be."

If I'd expected my words to wound him, I was dead wrong. The gentle smile was back, a rebuke more, I guessed, for himself than me. "I can't, ma'am."

"What do you mean?"

"I can't. My wings are changing. I can no longer fly."

"Then walk. The rest of us manage." I turned, but the firm grip of his dimly glowing hand on my shoulder stopped me. I yanked my shoulder away from his grasp, from the charged, arm-hair raising jolt of static that shot through me at his touch, and faced him again.

"I'm sorry, ma'am," he said, before I could give him a piece of my mind concerning personal boundaries, "but I am not like the others. I cannot just check out when I feel ready. For reasons even I don't understand, I am bound here until the change is complete."

I studied his wings, the mass of pale feathers dripping like twin spouts of water from his back. They didn't flicker like the rest of him. They had the first time I saw him, I was sure of it. And though they were etched with long, close lines like the raven's feathers, the points of them seemed sharper. I thought of the scissors sound they had made closing, and shuddered.

Thaddeus sensed my fear, and he spoke even more gently than before, as if afraid I might run screaming. "I do not wish to cause you any stress. I will leave as soon as I am able, I promise. I, too, would that I could move on, to wherever that may be."

I stood up straighter. I had an audience, after all, peering through the window. Maybe even listening in with some kind of ghostly power of extra-sensitive hearing, for all I knew. Either way, it wouldn't do for me to be seen losing control of my own house. "Then you will stay out of my yard and keep to your room until I am back from the hospital. I don't want you upsetting the others. No trouble, or I will find a way to make you leave, if I have to carry you out myself. Do you understand?"

His deep, flickering eyes didn't blink as they studied my face. "Yes, ma'am." Then he tilted his head to the sky, as if he heard a message from above. I gritted my teeth, hearing nothing, and walked back inside. The ghosts backed away as I entered, a transparent sea parting for a very peeved and frightened Moses. The phone began ringing, startling me further.

"Oh, for the love," I muttered, taking a deep breath before answering.

It was Tom. "Carol, come back right away. I think Rick's starting to wake up."

As I hung up I saw Thaddeus watching me, and by his expression it was clear he had heard Tom's words, long seconds before even I had. I rushed to the hospital and arrived in time to hear Rick, his eyes wide and frantic, babbling about someone appearing out of nowhere in front of his car, until he became so agitated that the nurses sent more of the clear, sleep-inducing fluid back through the tangle of tubes.

"Wings," he had said, over and over, sleepily once his eyes started to close. "He had black wings . . ."

I want him gone," I said, all doubt gone. "I don't care if he's molting or if this change is some kind of angelic menopause. I'm done with it."

Tom frowned, settling his sizeable bulk further into the small hospital chair that looked about as ready to call it quits as I was. "But Rick was clearly talking about black wings, which you said Thaddeus's aren't."

I thought of the raven again, of that beady-eyed stare. A dark pit settled in my stomach, which I fought to ignore.

"Rick wasn't talking *clearly* at all. He said he saw wings, before the accident, that he saw someone with wings. Black wings, yeah, but how do I know he can't make them any color he wants? How do I know anything about him? I want him gone, Tom. Tonight."

Tom pondered this for a moment, then shrugged. "Okay. It's been awhile since I've been able to pound some supernatural heads. I should go back and change into my vestments first, though."

"Is that really necessary?"

"If I'm going to send some creature back to hell, I'm going to do it like a proper priest, not as some schlub in a polo shirt."

Tom's sense of drama had always been irritating, but this time that wasn't what bothered me. "Do you think he'd go to hell? What if I'm wrong and he's a decent guy after all, what if . . ." I put my head in my hands. "Damn it, I just want him gone. I don't want to be responsible for where."

My brother's face softened. He knew my feelings on cuss words, and that things were bad if I used them. He leaned forward, and spoke in the voice I imagined he used to comfort his parishioners. "Carol, much as I love a good demonic beat-down, I won't do anything drastic unless he refuses to see reason. Besides, if he really is an angel—one on our side, that is—then the worst he'll have to worry about is having to towel off some holy water."

I considered this and nodded. At least with Tom, I had some back-up. Of course, this left Rick alone at the hospital, which was something I hated to do. I chided myself for it. Rick was a guy who liked his personal space. He'd probably hate the thought of me hovering over him constantly. The best thing I could do for him would be to let him have a few hours with ESPN in the background.

At least, that's what I told myself. I kissed his forehead like he did for me every evening after work, and squeezed his hand, which I barely ever touched anymore. His fingers were tough and calloused, though I didn't know whether it was more from air-conditioner repair or gardening.

"I'll be back soon," I said.

His chest moved up and down steadily. It was comforting, that movement. Something that felt like it would never change. Though I, more than anyone, knew that anything could change, at any time.

I felt Tom's hands on my shoulders. "He'll be fine, Carol."

I nodded. "I know."

Because God had already taken Shawn from me,

and by doing so, had already taken so much of Rick from me. And even I didn't think He was enough of a bastard to finish the job.

I waited in the car as Tom headed into the rectory, and stared at the church, trying to remember the last time I'd actually gone in.

Not going didn't mean not believing, however. It's a bit hard to be skeptical about the afterlife when you've got ghosts renting out rooms in your house on a regular basis. But I couldn't bring myself into that building, not since Shawn died. Six long years. Not because I would feel judged, though I often thought I deserved to be. But because doing so would remind me even more that Shawn hadn't just died. He had killed himself, and I knew the official religious stance on such things. Tom assured me that God knew us more than we knew ourselves, that He would measure Shawn's trials, his weaknesses. Like maybe God grades on a grand cosmic bell curve. It sure sounded good, but I saw lost souls every day in my current line of work. So obviously some still managed to fail the final exam.

Every time a guest checked out, their faces drawn in sorrow and a kind of confused fear, I worried that it would be Shawn who checked in next. Because even though I would see him again, I would know for sure that he was like the others. To this day, I still didn't know what drove my mostly sweet, often quiet, occasionally sarcastic, baseball and video game-loving boy to decide he couldn't handle his life anymore.

But knowing he was one of the guests in my hotel

for the damned would be enough to convince me I was done handling mine.

I was just adding these morose thoughts to my long list of reasons why I should abandon the hotel altogether and move to Florida like any self-respecting early retiree, when Tom joined me in the car. I must admit, he certainly looked more authoritative in the priestly frock. If he did get the chance to perform a movie-worthy hotel exorcism, he'd at least look the part.

It was well past dark by the time we returned home. No lights were on inside, though I could see the glow of a television set through the curtains in guest room two. I felt bad about forgetting to leave the lights on for my guests, but then remembered they were ghosts, not pets, and perfectly capable of working a light switch. Jinks was the one I should feel sorry for.

When I opened the door and turned on the hallway light, I saw Thaddeus standing in the doorway to the kitchen, as if he'd stood motionless in that same spot for the last several hours. Which was disturbing, and another reason to have him gone. I'd had enough of disturbing to last a lifetime.

"I thought I told you to keep to your room," I said. Tom filed in behind me, and out of the corner of my eye, I saw him puff up his chest in a way that was undoubtedly meant to look imposing, but only highlighted how much resistance to dieting ran in our family.

Thaddeus didn't seem to notice Tom. "I was watching, ma'am. I fear there is another about, one who is not like I am. One who perhaps has been here for some time now."

I felt like Diet Coke had been piped into my

veins, fizzy-alert and ice cold. "What do you mean? Would you please talk like a normal person?"

Tom put his hand on my arm, trying to calm me. "Carol tells me you claim to be an angel of God."

Thaddeus regarded Tom for the first time, those deep, transparent eyes taking in my brother. "I have not claimed to be anything." I noticed he still wasn't wearing his trench coat, as if he had decided the hotel was suddenly a wings-friendly locale. His wings looked changed even from a few hours ago, though the dim yellow hallway bulb could be the cause. They looked smoother, like the feathers had begun fusing together. They were not, however, black.

"Would you tell me what you *are*, exactly, Mr. Harper?" I cut back in. Tom may have been the priest, but this was still my house.

"I no longer know."

"Why don't you make a guess?"

He sighed. I hadn't realized I had the power to make an angel feel persecuted, but Rick probably wouldn't have been surprised. "I was an angel, as you say. But time, and pain, changes even us sometimes. And I am no longer what I was. I do not know what I am becoming, but I belong here. With the rest of them." He gestured behind him, to where several ghostly heads craned around the corner, watching the action. And here I thought a fresh bar of soap to sniff every so often was enough for a bunch of ghosts. Apparently what really attracted them was drama.

Seeing my glare, the guests filed silently back down the hallway. Within half a minute, the woman in room three was back to sobbing about Stanley again. It made things feel slightly more normal.

"Come on, let's sit and talk about this some more," Tom said, generously offering the use of my living room like it was his church office and Thaddeus some repentant congregant. I could tell that the head-busting idea had been put on the back burner for now.

Thaddeus was polite enough to only accept his offer at my irritated nod. We all sat.

"I've never met an angel before," Tom said. "So tell me, in Corinthians, when Paul says—"

"Tom," I warned. He wasn't here for a rousing scripture discussion.

"Right." He cleared his throat. "So you're no longer an angel? How is that possible?"

Thaddeus looked down at his hands, which were steepled together in his lap. They looked like they would be strong hands, and maybe calloused, like Rick's. "I have been among humanity for many, many centuries, for time longer than time itself remembers. And I have ministered and I have guarded and I have recorded, like others of my kind."

"Recorded?"

"It is one of our tasks, to remember and record in the Book of Life. And for as long as I have existed, I have fulfilled my duties. But lately . . ." he trailed off, and I couldn't help but lean in, captivated by his words. Did angels get bored at work, too? Did they want a holiday from the whole ministering and recording gig?

"Lately, I have been unable to. I have begun feeling the pain around me. I have felt the hopelessness and the fear and the sorrow deep in my bones, in a way that I never have in so many centuries of time. I could no longer continue my work among the others, or even to *be* among them, so bright and full of the hope and light that I lost more of each day."

There was a beat of silence. I frowned. "That's it? You started feeling what it was like to be a human?"

"And I am ceasing to be an angel."

"But what about God?" Tom asked. "As an angel of Heaven, surely your faith in Him was enough. Angels aren't susceptible to human folly, to—"

"To falling? We all are tested, Father Hannigan. Our purpose is not always clear. Sometimes even those such as I can no longer go on."

Tom appeared taken aback, though whether at his argument or at Thaddeus knowing his name, I couldn't tell.

"So you're *damned*, then? You feel a little pain, maybe a little doubt, and you get sent here to join the rest of the lost souls? That's a crappy retirement package," I said. I realized that I was offended on Thaddeus's behalf, despite only ten minutes ago being ready to toss him out on his angelic butt. How did he do that?

He looked at me curiously. "No one is sent here," he said. "Whether they know why or not, they all come of their own free will. They are drawn here, like I was. Pain seeks out itself."

I tried to sort through what that meant and if I should be angry about it, when Tom cut back in. "What is this other thing you talked about? The one you were watching for? Does he have black wings? Because if he was the one who hurt Rick, his ass is toast."

There was the Tom I knew, ready to whip out the holy water and the unimaginative cussing.

"There are others, our opposites, angels of the Betrayer. I have sensed one nearby, though I do not understand why or what business he would have here."

Where hope is already lost, I thought.

"Rick said he saw someone with black wings, just before he crashed," Tom said.

"They do not directly interfere in such ways with humanity. They prey on thoughts, desires, weaknesses. The opposite of the ministering that I and those like me perform. But perhaps he wanted it to appear that he did, for some reason I cannot fathom."

I watched carefully. Tom continued to question Thaddeus about types of angels, the whole good, bad, and ugly of the situation, but something continued to worry at me. Finally, I spoke my doubt outright. "How do we know, Mr. Harper, that you aren't one of these 'other' angels? How do we know this isn't all some trick, that you can't make yourself appear however or wherever you like? How do we know we can trust you?"

"I think he's telling the truth, Carol. My perpsense isn't tingling," Tom offered. But I ignored him and his supposed perp sense. I wanted to hear it from Thaddeus.

"You can't know for sure," he said after a moment. "But if you do not believe me, and you wish me to leave, you can force me to."

My suspicion rose. "You said before that you couldn't leave. That you were bound here, whatever that means."

"I cannot leave on my own, not until my wings have finished their change, until I have finished *my* change into whatever it is I will become, spirit or lost soul or nothing but air. But you can make me leave. You can shatter my wings."

"What?"

"They grow more fragile by the moment, becoming

something separate from me. I do not know how I know so surely, but when they are gone, so am I."

This was unexpected. "And you are telling me this because . . ."

"If you truly cannot trust me, you can make me leave. You must have that choice."

I eyed the wings again, folded tightly against his back. The light of the lamp reflected off them, making his back appear to glow yellow. They were lovely, in a crystalline sort of way, and smashing them seemed horrible, like breaking the windows of a church. I wasn't violent by nature, had even balked at spanking Shawn when he dumped that red nail polish on the dining room carpet.

But the knowledge that I could do it, if necessary, was reassuring.

"Fine," I said. "So what do we do about the other one?"

Even Thaddeus didn't seem to have an answer for that.

It was decided that Tom would stay at the hospital with Rick, and after he performed some sort of blessing involving fancy Latin words and a liberal sprinkling of holy water, he seemed confident the house would be safe from any fiends of hell. Thaddeus still appeared troubled, but didn't say anything.

Tom left for the hospital, and Thaddeus went to his room. I sat in the living room awhile longer, letting Jinks wind his way around my legs.

"Miss Carol?" a female voice said, interrupting my thoughts. The woman from room three. Her voice had a hitch to it, probably from all the crying.

"Yes, uh . . .," I started, realizing I'd still never looked up her name.

"Barbara." She scowled at having to remind me.

"Yes, Barbara. What's wrong?" The ghosts never approached me to talk. Ever.

"I heard him earlier, in his room. It sounded like he was talking to someone."

"What do you mean? Like praying?"

She shook her head, and her chins quivered along with her big roller-curled hair. "I thought I heard a voice talking back. A child's. Reminded me of my Stanley, back when we were young."

I sat there, chilled. A child's voice. In guest room one, Shawn's old room. I didn't know what to believe, or if I even could anymore.

"Thank you for telling me."

She started silently back to her room, and I couldn't help but blurt out, "So who is Stanley?" It surprised even me that I would ask. I had taken a very "live and let live" approach with my guests. They didn't ask personal information about me, and I didn't run any post-mortem background checks on them.

The woman seemed to deflate again, in that strange way she had at the table last night. "He's the only person who ever loved me. And I made his life miserable for it."

And with that she slunk back into her room, though I didn't hear any crying for the rest of the night.

I spent most of the next week at the hospital with Rick, and so I didn't hear much from either the ghosts or Thaddeus. Tom, bless his generous, priestly soul, continued to take the hospital night shift. Rick had been recovering remarkably well and we hadn't seen so much as a black feather to indicate otherworldly trouble. Even the raven hadn't shown up around the yard. I was beginning to think we had overreacted.

Then again, I lived with ghosts and a semi-fallen angel, so I suppose a little paranoia was understandable.

Rick, for his part, was back to his usual coherent, though not particularly talkative, self. Much of my time at the hospital was spent watching some sport or another with him, and making the occasional run to summon a nurse for more grape jello. Tom and I filled him in on all that had happened with Thaddeus, before and since the car crash, all of which Rick took in remarkable stride. Most likely, he was just tucking all this in the part of his brain labeled "denial," where anything regarding us running a hotel for lost souls usually resided. Rick didn't even remember seeing anyone with black wings in the accident or talking about it afterward. The doctor said some short term memory loss was not surprising, given the blow to the head Rick received, and I guess that particular memory wouldn't be the worst one to lose. Plus, now that he was healing better than anyone could have hoped for, I could amuse myself with the notion that bringing up Rick's "blow to the head" would help me settle many a future argument.

"They say I'll get to go home by Saturday," Rick said, fiddling with the plastic fork as if debating whether he was hungry enough to actually eat the food on his tray.

I raised an eyebrow, looking up from the regency romance novel I hadn't been paying much attention to anyway. "They seem to think I'll take you back."

Rick smiled. It wasn't the huge, silly grin he used to give so freely, like when Shawn would tell one of his made-up knock-knock jokes, but I was content with it. I think after Shawn died, this new, tight smile was all he had left.

"Have you been keeping an eye on my roses?"

"Mmmmmm," I said noncommittally. I scanned over the book again, though I didn't think I had read any words in it for the last several pages.

"Wonderful. With as hot as it's been, the entire lot of them are probably gone by now."

"How do you know how hot it's been?" I asked. "You've been sitting around indoors being pampered for a week now."

"I fix air-conditioners. It's my job to know. And have you tasted this food? This isn't pampered. This is a slow assassination."

I chuckled, then realized that this was one of the better conversations Rick and I had had in months. That thought made me sigh.

Rick chewed on a bite of something involving rice and a brown sauce. "What?" he asked.

I didn't want to tell him the reason behind my sigh. But there was something I needed to bring up, though I knew it would sour the current good mood.

I set the book down in my lap. "Do you ever hear Shawn? In the house, I mean. Well, not Shawn so much as the memory of Shawn. I mean . . ." I sighed again. I wasn't fully sure what I meant. I tensed, waiting for the inevitable shut-down. Rick wasn't a man to talk about his feelings, particularly when it came to his dead son.

Rick chewed some more, as if he had found a particularly tough bite. And, well, he probably had. "I know what you mean."

"You do?"

"You know that bat of his?" Rick looked down at

his plate, shuffling around some wilted green beans with his fork.

"Yeah," I said. "His little league bat."

"Sometimes at night, when you're asleep, I take it out in the yard. I practice a few swings with it, you know, pretend I'm showing him how it's done again."

I swallowed, blinking against the tears that threatened to start.

"And every once in a while, it's like I can hear him there, with me," Rick continued, barely above a whisper. "Sometimes he's just a little boy again, sometimes he's all grown up, ready to leave for college. It's not like with the . . . the guests, you know. He's not really there. But . . . it's nice."

I hadn't ever known this, hadn't ever imagined Rick out in the backyard, playing baseball with the memory of our son.

"It's nice," I agreed. And because I couldn't think of anything else to do, I reached over and held his hand. His calloused fingers wrapped around mine, and we stared at the announcer of some post-game event on the T.V. Neither of us bothered wiping away the tears trailing down our cheeks.

Saturday came, and Tom and I brought Rick home, though he protested needing our help to walk from the car into the house. We settled him into our bedroom, where, despite his claims of being perfectly fine, the exertion of leaving the hospital left him asleep within moments of laying down.

The guests, thankfully, stayed out of sight inside

their bedrooms while we brought Rick in the house. Once the bedroom door was closed, though, Marco and Mr. Kirman drifted back out to resume their game of gin rummy in the dining room.

"This group seems more social than the others," Tom commented, watching the mostly silent card game take place.

"They're regular party animals," I said.

He had a point, though. Something about this group was different lately. I wasn't sure whether it was due to the disaster of a dinner conversation last week, Thaddeus's presence, or maybe my absence for long stretches during the day. But when I would come home from the hospital, I would often find two or three of them in hushed conversation. Add that to Barbara talking to me out of the blue a few nights ago, and Marco asking yesterday if we had any board games they could play, and I could safely say that something had changed. Or maybe, like Thaddeus, it was in the process of changing, though to what, I couldn't say. I did, however, manage to find not only a pack of cards for Marco, but also Shawn's old favorite game, Battleship. It may have been missing a destroyer and two submarines, but I had never seen a ghost get so excited before, like I had just handed him a dusty, battered box containing all of Christmas.

"I haven't seen Thaddeus around since we talked with him," Tom said. "How is he?" Tom may have been concerned, but I knew him well enough to know that he was also itching to sit the angel down for a big old religious question and answer session.

"He's been keeping to himself." I hadn't seen him much myself in the evenings. But last night, when I'd walked past his room, the door was slightly ajar.

I looked in, much like I had when I first spied those huge, once-feathery wings.

This time, though, the angel was on his knees on the floor. Like he was praying, maybe, but his arms were wrapped around himself, and he rocked back and forth. He himself was more transparent, the flicker more dramatic than I had ever seen. His wings were almost completely smooth, two broad, thin sheets like ice on his back. He let out a little moan, and I had jumped away.

If Thaddeus had been what he claimed, how could God let this happen to him? To one of His own angels?

I knew I should tell Tom, but there was nothing my brother could do but worry. And maybe pray, though if it didn't work for Thaddeus, I didn't think it would for any of us.

"And nothing from the son of a bitch devil that hurt Rick?" Tom's voice brought me back from the horrible image.

I shook my head. No news is good news, they say, but I don't think that necessarily applies to having angels of Satan hovering around the neighborhood.

"Well, call me the second you hear anything. I've got a bag full of crosses, and a super-soaker loaded up with holy water already in my car."

I smiled and impulsively threw my arms around my brother. "You're a good man, Tom. One of the best. Despite the cussing."

He hugged me back. "Damn right."

C arol, it's almost time. The change is becoming complete, I can feel it."

I looked up from the groceries I was unloading on the table after a run to the store later that evening.

"Mr. Harper, are you all right?" I felt stupid the minute the words left my mouth. Of course he was not all right. His whole body, with the exception of those wings, seemed to flicker completely in and out of existence. His face, when I could see it, was etched with lines of pain I couldn't even comprehend. The static feeling was stronger, too. The hairs on my arms stood up from his presence, even from across the room.

"I need your help. Please. I cannot make the change on my own. I know that now. It is you that must . . .," he trailed off with a low groan.

My mouth, already open, gaped further. A new bar of soap— cherry blossom, by request of Mrs. Li—slipped from my fingers and hit the floor. "Help you?"

"I told you how to do it. It is the only way."

"Rick!" I called, desperately. Surely this was something we could work through. I couldn't smash those wings, those beautiful, terrible wings. Wouldn't that be like killing him? Condemning him like the rest of them? The rest of us? "Rick, I need your help!"

"Carol," Thaddeus said quietly, and all those ages of time untold he had lived through filled his voice. His lips strained through agony to form a smile. "Please. I know this is what I must do. I was wrong. I *was* sent here, after all. There is a purpose for me, a glorious purpose. But you have to help me check out. Before the other—" A groan cut off the rest of his words.

I shook my head, backing up until my hip hit the kitchen island. And then my legs gave out altogether.

Shawn was standing there, in the door frame between the kitchen and the living room.

Shawn. *Oh God, my Shawn. My son.*

"Mom, you can't trust him," Shawn said, and I knew this was no errant memory, that this was his voice, and his face. He was grayish and slightly transparent, just like my guests, but he was Shawn, just as he had been that last weekend he came home from school to do his laundry and eat a home-cooked meal and toss a ball around in the backyard with Rick. The last weekend he had ever come home.

"Shawn! Oh, Shawn . . ." I struggled to get to my feet, but my limbs wouldn't cooperate. Then Shawn's hands were pulling me up, those strong hands with long fingers that always made me think that he should've played piano, and my arms were wrapped around the ghost of my son, and I was sobbing.

"Carol," Thaddeus said. I barely registered that he was still there. What was a dying angel compared to my son, here and in my arms? "Carol, please."

Shawn pulled back, and I could barely see his face through the blur of tears. "Mom, you have to listen to me. He's not an angel. He's trying to trick you."

"What?" I couldn't focus on his words, I was so enraptured by the sight of his face.

"It's a trick. He's the one with the black wings. He's the one who hurt Dad. He's a demon. An angel of hell. And if you do what he wants, if you break his wings, he'll be free."

That hit home. I turned to stare at Thaddeus, betrayal stabbing at my heart. Could it be? Was

117

Thaddeus the other one all this time, playing on my sympathies?

Just then I heard a sound, a kind of guttural cry, and I saw Rick standing in the hallway. A metal baseball bat, Shawn's bat, was in his hands, probably the closest thing to grab for self-defense when he'd heard my desperate call, before he limped his way to my rescue.

He stood there, frozen in awe and disbelief. "Shawn?"

Shawn kept his eyes on mine. "Mom, he'll be gone soon. God will send him back where he belongs, far from you and Dad. But you can't help him, or everything's lost."

"I—I don't . . .," I stammered.

"Carol," Thaddeus said again, and flickered out of existence for a full second before coming back, "Carol, trust me, please. That is—" Flicker out. Flicker back. A grimace of agony, a moan, before he began again, "It's not Shawn. Shawn won't be coming here, not to the hotel."

I squeezed my son's hand—ghostly, yes, but real. Thaddeus was lying. He'd been lying all along. Shawn nodded, as if he could hear my thoughts, and still holding my hand, he led me from the kitchen, away from Thaddeus Harper slowly dying whatever death came to immortals.

"Shawn?" Rick tried again, inching closer, holding onto the wall as if that alone was keeping him up-right. I understood the feeling. "Is it really you?"

"Yeah, Dad. It's me."

Thaddeus stumbled from the kitchen clutching his chest, doubled over from the weight of his wings, that now-solid sheet of pure crystal covering his back like a shield. "He lies. He is not your son," he moaned, falling to his knees beside the armchair. Behind him I saw the other four guests, watching the scene unfold with various expressions of ghostly horror. Mr. Kirman even had his arm around Mrs. Li, who appeared to be crying.

I put my hands up over my eyes, unable to take the sight of it, of Thaddeus, even if he was an angel of hell, dying in agony in front of me.

"Carol," Thaddeus continued, his voice a broken whisper. "Please. The reason I knew—" Flicker out, flicker in. I couldn't see it anymore, but I could feel it happening. "I knew what to do because your little boy told me. Shawn, the memory of Shawn—" Flicker out, flicker in. "I saw a memory of Shawn in his room, talking to you." Flicker out, flicker in, moan. "He . . . he said, 'Mommy, I need help, I can't . . . I can't break it myself, I can't set them free.' " Flicker out, flicker in. "He was talking about a—" Flicker out.

I removed my hands. "A pack of baseball cards. His first pack of baseball cards. Rick said that baseball players were in there, and Shawn thought there were real people trapped inside." And Rick and I had laughed so hard about it later that night, lying together in bed. Our precocious, sensitive little boy.

"It's almost over, Mom. It'll be okay," Shawn said, smiling that sweet, slightly crooked smile at me.

And that's when I knew. Because it looked like Shawn's smile, to the very last detail, but I remembered more about Shawn's smile than the shape of his lips and the half-dimple that formed in his chin. I knew how it made me feel, on those rare occasions when my serious, usually deep-in-thought son flashed me one of those beautiful smiles.

And when this Shawn smiled, I felt nothing.

I stepped away from him, away from this imposter,

my insides turned to ice.

Thaddeus flickered back in, and a scream of pain ripped from him. Barbara covered her ears and wailed along with him, and soon the rest of the ghosts joined in, a haunting choir of pain.

"Rick!" I yelled, holding out my hand. And for the first time in years, my husband could read my thoughts. He set his jaw grimly, and tossed me Shawn's baseball bat.

Shawn, who was not Shawn, began to change. The image of my son slid off like a snake shedding skin, and a set of jet black wings stretched out, so wide they reached from wall to wall. Oily black, gleaming like the wings of the raven, because they were the same, just made larger. The being standing in front of me was nothing like Thaddeus, nothing like the ghosts, nothing like any creature I had ever seen. He was tall, stretching almost to the ceiling, with cruel red eyes and a thin face angled so sharply his cheekbones could be weapons. Dark purple veins pulsed under paper-white skin. His smile was now nothing at all like Shawn's. Blood-red lips sneered over jagged, knife-like teeth, vicious and triumphant.

But I was no longer afraid. This thing had pretended to be my son. He had made me think, just for a few moments, that Shawn was back in my arms, and he had ripped him away from me again.

Thaddeus looked up at me and saw the bat in my hands. He smiled, peace shining through the agony, because he knew I finally got it.

Pain seeks out itself, Thaddeus had said, and he was right. The demon, the raven, which had been here for years, possibly ever since Shawn's death, preying on my pain and Rick's and the lost souls'.

Drowning us all slowly in our own sorrow.

Somewhere in my mind I could hear a small child's voice. Shawn's voice, like an echo from the past. "Set them free, Mommy," he said.

But before I could, the demon let out a roar of fury so deafening I stumbled back into the couch, while the ghosts screamed and screamed. I felt black wings sweeping down to enfold me, smelled the stench of rot and ash, and then there was a flash of crystal before me.

Thaddeus. He lunged into the demon, and the two were locked together, but only briefly. Flicker out.

I kicked over the cheap end table and the lamp tumbled off. I needed room to swing.

Flicker in.

I remembered how I had seen Shawn do it, and Rick, so many times, playing in the backyard under that tree I could no longer look at. I may have been middle-aged and overweight, and the last person anyone sane would pick for their team, but I was a mom and I was mad as hell. I swung with everything in me.

The big, solid wing that was no longer a wing at all, but its own separate, mirror-like entity, cracked and shattered. Huge chunks of it fell to the carpet. Light, brilliant white and so blinding I had to shield my eyes, poured from Thaddeus's back, enveloping both angel and demon entirely. The demon roared one last time, but the light was so bright, so pure, that nothing of darkness could ever hope to withstand it.

Hope, I thought then, crazily. *That's what hope feels like.*

The light surged to fill the whole room, and then it was gone, and both Thaddeus and the demon were gone with it. Rick and I and our four ghosts were left behind, blinking and trembling in the living room, which was dark now, except for the light from the kitchen and the toppled-over lamp.

No one dared speak. Barbara started making that hiccupping sound like she might begin to cry for Stanley, but nothing came out.

Then Rick, bless him, said, "Good swing, Carol." And I ran to him and fell into his arms, and we both sobbed and laughed, unable to decide on one or the other.

The ghosts let us be for several moments, but then Mr. Kirman said, in his thin, hesitant voice. "Where do you think he went? Thaddeus?"

Mrs. Li bent down and picked up a slim, jagged piece of glass. "His wings did not disappear."

"Well, why on earth—" Barbara from room three started, looking down at a piece of glass wing at her feet. She gasped.

"Stanley!" she cried, her hands flying to her massive cheeks. "Oh, my Stanley! How . . .?"

She picked up the glass, tears streaming down her face. She stared at it, mesmerized, and then she, like Thaddeus in that last moment I had seen his face, looked at once happy and at peace, despite all the pain she had been through. She clutched the piece of glass to her chest, and the light came back, softer this time, until her whole form was filled with it. And then she vanished.

Mrs. Li, too, gasped, seeing something in her own piece of glass. She looked vaguely stunned as the light enveloped her. In the last moment I saw her, her mouth was a small "o" of surprise.

Marco was next, and he laughed at whatever he saw in his shard of wing, looking happier even than when I had pulled out Battleship.

Mr. Kirman was the last, and he straightened himself a bit before he looked into his own glass, as if he wanted to prepare himself for what he might see. He peered into it, and a shy smile crept over his face. As the light poured over him, he gave Rick and me a small wave. Then he, too, disappeared.

Rick and I stood there, alone in our house for the first time in five years. Our home. Deep inside, I knew that it was finally that again. There would be no more lost souls here, living or dead. Just us, and the chance to start again. The chance to really live, for the first time in six years. He kissed my forehead, and I held him tighter.

There was one shard of wing left, for us, and I was pretty sure who we would see inside. I couldn't wait to see his smile.

Acknowledgments

So many people have helped in shaping these stories and making this book possible, and I wish I could make a cup of hot chocolate (Hal's store brand, of course) for each and every one of you. But as that would prove difficult (not the least of which because Hal's is a fictional grocery store), I guess I'll have to settle with thanking you the good ol' fashioned way.

Thank you to my many beta readers over the years— The Damn Triangle (Greg, Gama, Sarah, Ken, Chris and Jeff), and to my writing group (Bryce, Dantzel, Kristy, Chris, Lesley, Bradley, and Holly) and to all the others who have read and commented on my stories and, in doing so, helped me become a better writer. Huge thanks to Kristina Kugler for her amazing editing expertise, and also to David Farland, Janci Patterson, and Nancy Fulda for loving my work enough to give me such fabulous cover quotes.

Thank you to the editors and publishers who originally deemed these stories worthy of inclusion in their publications—to Brian White and the team at *Fireside Magazine,* to Lisa Mangum and the WordFire Press team, and to the folks in charge of *Sibyl's Scriptorium*. Knowing that such talented (and obviously discerning) folk such as yourselves loved my stories enough to publish them gave me the confidence I needed to keep writing more.

Thank you to Galen Dara for the incredible illustration she did for "Tuesdays with Molakesh the Destroyer" when it was first published in *Fireside Magazine* (and which I was able to use for the cover of this anthology) and also to Holly Heisey for the fantastic cover design.

Thank you to Dantzel, Lauren, Nancy, and Janci, who have all been there for me in countless ways in my writing career, as well as just being the most amazing friends who make my life more awesome in general. Love you ladies like crazy!

Most of all, thank you to my family, both those I am related to and those I married into. To Mom and Dad, who handed me my first fantasy book (Lord of the Rings), bought me my first computer (RIP, Chomps) and never stopped believing in me. And especially to my husband and kids, who support me through it all. I love you beyond words.

Megan Grey lives in Utah with her husband, two kids, and two dogs (all of whom are incredibly supportive of the time she spends writing about retired demons and other supernatural outcasts). When not writing or chasing her kids around, she spends much of her free time making medieval Barbie dioramas. Her fiction can be found in *Fireside* magazine, *One Horn to Rule Them All: A Purple Unicorn Anthology*, and *Sibyl's Scriptorium*. To find out more about Megan, visit her website at megangrey.com.

www.ingramcontent.com/pod-product-compliance
Lightning Source LLC
Chambersburg PA
CBHW020739130626
46554CB00006B/2060